GLEN LANIER

THE
ROUGHRIDER

Complete and Unabridged

LINFORD
Leicester

First published in Great Britain in 2005 by
Robert Hale Limited
London

First Linford Edition
published 2006
by arrangement with
Robert Hale Limited
London

British Library CIP Data

Lanier, Glen
    The roughrider.—Large print ed.—
Linford western library
1. Western stories
2. Large type books
I. Title
823.9'2 [F]

ISBN 1–84617–205–5

Published by
F. A. Thorpe (Publishing)
Anstey, Leicestershire

Set by Words & Graphics Ltd.
Anstey, Leicestershire
Printed and bound in Great Britain by
T. J. International Ltd., Padstow, Cornwall

This book is printed on acid-free paper

THE ROUGHRIDER

It is 1902 and Captain Buck Buchanan, Spanish-American war veteran, is travelling to New Mexico Territory to visit friends. He rescues a beautiful young woman, Emily Valdez, from outlaws hired by businessmen who want her father's land. But when it comes to light that Buck's friends are in on the fraudulent land deal, the pair find themselves with no allies . . . Heavily outnumbered by conspirators and henchmen, they must make a last stand against all the odds.

1

Ernesto Valdez drank in the cool, mountain air as he drove his team of horses through a winding canyon deep in the heart of the Pecos high country in northern New Mexico. His daughter, Emily sat on the wagon seat beside him. As he had done countless times before, he found himself wishing his wife was alive to see the woman their daughter had become. She had her mother's dark beauty and flashing green eyes.

Valdez was delivering supplies to one of his sheep camps. This one was four days out, by wagon, just above timberline at the head of the Rio Maestos. The last three days had been fun for both father and daughter. As Valdez guided his team up and down mountains and through canyons, he pointed out many interesting features of the land to Emily and told her folk stories he had learned as a boy in the sheep camps of his father.

Suddenly, the sound of running horses filled the canyon like the low rumble of a spring thunderstorm. A large group of riders swept out of the trees on the right of the meadow and headed straight for the wagon.

'Papa, who are they?' Emily's voice trembled with fear.

'Youngblood,' Valdez said through clinched teeth.

'What's he want of us?' Many stories were told in the Mexican community about the outlaw, Clay Youngblood. He was known to be a vicious killer. The mysterious disappearance of many sheepherders and cowboys was blamed on him.

'I don't know, but let's find out.' Valdez reined in his team, then bent down and pulled his old and worn Winchester from under the wagon seat and laid it across his lap. He couldn't outrun Clay and his gang. He only regretted that he had brought Emily along.

Emily shut her eyes and took several deep breaths, trying to control the waves of fear washing over her. She opened her eyes just as one rider went to the front of the wagon's team. Another stopped on her side of the wagon, just behind her. She couldn't see him but she could hear his horse breathing and tossing its bit in its mouth. Five more riders drew up on her father's side.

'Good morning, Clay,' Valdez said, keeping his voice even, not betraying the fear churning in the pit of his stomach. Youngblood had changed. He looked older and more prosperous since Valdez had found him wounded and dying. That was eight, maybe ten years ago, back when Valdez was still doing some sheep herding himself. Valdez had patched him up and carried him back to camp where he nursed him back to health. Youngblood never said how he came to be in such bad shape and Valdez knew not to ask. Two weeks later, he returned to his camp after a

3

hard day and found Youngblood gone. Some of Valdez's food was missing as was his spare rifle, an old single shot, and a box of shells. The same day a neighboring herder was murdered and his horse stolen. Many times since, Valdez thought how much better off everyone would be if he had let the outlaw die.

'*Buenos dias*, Ernesto,' the outlaw said. He touched his hat and smiled at Emily. But there was no smile in his eyes. His gaze from under the hat brim was cold and without any emotion. Emily shuddered.

'Going to your sheep camp, Ernesto?'

'*Sí.*' Valdez noted how the outlaws moved from behind Youngblood and out of the line of fire.

'I have a message for you from the colonel. He thinks you should reconsider his offer to buy your spread up on the Chama.'

'Tell Russell that there's nothing to reconsider,' Valdez said. Russell had been pressuring and trying to bully him into selling this small ranch for over a year. Valdez now owned a larger ranch south-east of Sante Fe, but the Chama land was the homeplace of Valdez's family. His father's father had been born there, as had his father and himself. All his children had been born there. 'I won't sell and that's final.'

'You better listen up, you dumb Mexican!' a shrill, thin voice cut in. A rider on Youngblood's right stepped his horse closer to the wagon. 'Or something might happen to you or your family.'

Valdez looked closely at the rider and suddenly recognized him as J.W. Russell, the colonel's heir and would-be badman.

'Shut up, J.W.,' Youngblood hissed at the young man, 'I'll do the talking!'

'Clay, I knew you worked for Russell,' Valdez grinned at Youngblood, 'but I didn't know you had to baby-sit his piss-ant son too.'

'Piss-ant!' the young man screeched. 'Piss-ant? I'll show you who's a piss-ant!'

'Can we go now?' Valdez asked, ignoring the near hysterical J.W. Russell, and looking only at Youngblood.

'Lookout!' someone yelled, and then a gun went off.

Valdez clutched at his shoulder. Emily screamed as the bullet tore through her father and hit her, knocking her off the wagon. Youngblood looked around to see young Russell with his gun out trying to aim at Valdez for another shot. But Russell's horse was dancing around, frightened by the deafening explosion less than two feet from its ears.

'Get that gun away from him before he shoots one of us!' Youngblood yelled at his men. He turned back to Valdez in time to see the wounded man struggling to bring his rifle up to bear on J.W.

Youngblood didn't even stop to think about it. He had his own gun out before Valdez could take aim. Youngblood emptied his gun into Valdez.

Russell's horse was now totally spooked from all the shooting and started running out of control up the canyon. J.W., eyes wide with fright, was clutching the saddle horn and holding on for dear life. Youngblood spurred his horse into pursuit.

'Catch that little piss-ant before he gets hurt,' the outlaw yelled at his men. 'If anything happens to junior, the colonel will run us out of the country . . . or worse!'

★   ★   ★

Buck Buchanan lay behind a downed tree on the far side of a high mountain meadow. He watched through his rifle sights as a big buck moved noiselessly through the thicket of aspen ringing the small meadow. Every few steps it paused, listening to the sounds of the mountain and testing the early morning breeze with its wet nose. Even though the deer was only a few yards from the clearing's edge, Buck dared not shoot. A branch or small trunk might deflect his bullet.

Suddenly the buck stopped and jerked his head up. From the canyon below came the harsh crack of one and then several shots, their echoes reverberating off one mountainside to another, shattering the morning quiet. The animal wheeled, then plunged back through the aspen and quickly disappeared into the dark spruce behind. For a few seconds, Buck heard the deer crashing through the thick timber and then the mountain was again still.

For the past two mornings he had sat on the ridge opposite this one, watching through field-glasses as the buck came to graze in the meadow. It always arrived an hour after sunrise and stayed until mid-morning. Then it moved into the thick timber to bed down for the day. Today, since long before first light, Buck had lain in the cold, damp meadow grass behind the log, waiting and hoping the deer would come back a third time. Now, he was disappointed because all his work had been for nothing. And, there was also the shooting. He would have to make his way down the mountainside and cross that canyon to get back to his camp.

Buck stood up stiffly, stretching his limbs, which had become chilled from the early morning cold and dampness. He followed an old game trail that angled up the mountain. Several times he had to duck and crawl where the undergrowth was too low for his tall frame. Fifteen minutes later he came to a smaller meadow where he had left his horses tied to picket pins so they could graze on the meadow's lush grass.

His horses snorted in recognition as he came out in the meadow to gather them in. Alamo, his big dun, was saddled. Old Sarge, a large roan, carried an empty pack frame on which Buck had planned to haul out the deer. He tightened cinches on both horses and then slid his little carbine into the rifle boot hanging from his worn but highly polished saddle. Old habits were hard to break. Even though he was on extended leave from the army, Captain

Buck Buchanan still rigged the old McClellen saddle as if he were with a cavalry troop. Hanging ominously from the off side was his sabre.

★ ★ ★

The sides of the canyon were covered with thick stands of spruce and Douglas fir. Buck followed old game trails but progress was slow. It took him until noon to quietly work his way down to the foot of the mountain. The canyon bottom widened out here, to form a large meadow several hundred yards wide and maybe a half-mile long. A stream wound back and forth down its length. He reined in his horses and sat watching and listening from the cover of a small stand of ponderosa pines at the meadow's edge.

A hundred yards in front of him, out in the middle of the canyon, was a green and yellow buckboard wagon with the motionless body of a man sprawled across the seat. Even at that distance Buchanan could make out bloodstains on the man's white shirt. One of the two horses hitched to the wagon lay slumped in a heap. The other horse appeared to be unharmed and stood quietly.

For ten minutes Buck sat watching and listening. He studied the surrounding mountainsides and the canyon itself. Nothing moved. The only sounds were the sighing of the wind through the pines overhead and the raspy calls of ravens down the canyon. From a distance came the faint rumble of thunder from dark clouds building up over the mountain peaks to the west. Buck figured he had a half-hour at the most before the storm hit.

Satisfied that there was little danger from ambush, Buck tied his pack horse up short to a tree, pulled the carbine from its boot and laid it across the saddle pommel in front of him. Years of military service had taught him to always be prepared for the unexpected. He loosened the holster flap of his service revolver and then headed the dun out at a slow walk toward the wagon.

The body was that of a Mexican in his late forties or early fifties. The man had been shot four or five times. Buck got down and cut the unharmed horse loose and removed its harness. Maybe it would find its way home. At least it could get to feed and water now. He went back by the wagon and began studying tracks to sort out the story they told.

Patiently, track by track, he began to put together a story of what had happened here. It was the old story of an ambush. A party of horsemen had waited in the trees on the far side of the canyon, then swept down on the wagon and killed its driver. At that point the story blurred. For some reason, after attacking the wagon the riders headed north at a hard run, up the canyon. Nothing in the wagon seemed to have been disturbed.

As Buck studied the tracks, he suddenly came across a set of footprints too small to be those of a man; more like those made by a boy or a woman. And there were drops of blood. The small footprints led away from the wagon, toward the small stream that meandered through the canyon floor near the far side. Buchanan followed them in that direction.

He lost the tracks in the tall grass near the edge of the stream and knelt down to see better. As he did, he heard a twig snap directly behind him. Buck sprang up suddenly, turning and swinging his carbine like a club. It caught the end of a rifle barrel pointing straight at his chest and deflected it to one side just as the gun went off. The blast was deafening and made his ears ring. Buck grabbed the barrel and wrenched the rifle out of the hands of the figure holding it. To his surprise it was a woman. For a second she stood staring at him, her eyes wide with terror and her ashen face full of pain. Blood covered the front of her blouse. Then she collapsed at his feet.

Buck knelt beside her and ripped her blouse open. She had a bullet hole high up, through her shoulder. He couldn't find any signs of any other wounds. She must have fainted from shock and loss of blood. He tore strips of cloth from her skirt and, with practised hands, bandaged her wound. He had doctored many such wounds in Cuba, in the trenches high up on the ridges. There, in the sticky heat and humidity, the big killer hadn't been the wounds themselves, as much as the fever and infection, especially gangrene, which seemed to almost always follow later.

As he dressed the wound, he noticed that the woman was very pretty, and young, in her mid-twenties he guessed. About the same age as Alice, his fiancée, but with dark, blue-black hair. Alice, however, had fiery red hair, a color that matched her temperament.

The last time he had seen Alice, she had exploded when he told her he was going to postpone their wedding. He had hastily reassured her that he loved her but needed time to sort out whether or not he wanted to continue in the Army. Alice, the daughter of a major-general, had looked at Buck as if he had just lost his mind.

In a very controlled voice she reminded him that her daddy said that Buck was destined for great things in the Army. As she had dressed, she said he would be a fool to throw away such a promising career. And she pointed out that if he waited too long, he might just lose the love of a woman who could be of great help in that career. With that, she had flounced out of his hotel room. That had been a month ago, just days before he came West.

Buck forced his mind off Alice and back to the wounded girl. Perhaps she was the daughter of the man on the wagon. There were no rings on her fingers to indicate that she might be his wife. Whoever she was, Buck knew that he must get her to shelter if he hoped to save her. Thunderheads were rolling in over the canyon and in his brief time in these mountains, Buck had learned that afternoon showers were the rule.

There was also, Buck realized, another danger . . . the men who set the ambush. They might be coming back this way, perhaps soon. He had to work fast.

He found a shovel in the back of the wagon and dug a shallow grave, up near the ponderosas. After emptying the man's pockets, he half carried, half dragged the body over and buried it. Buck slashed a large blaze on the nearest tree to mark the grave's location.

After replacing the shovel and stowing the man's belongings in his saddle-bag, Buck led his horses out to the stream and watered them. Finally, he lifted the woman onto the dun, and got up behind her. He held the unconscious woman in his arms as they rode slowly across the canyon in the direction of his camp.

A few drops of rain fell from the massing dark clouds and thunder echoed off the surrounding mountains. Then, as the rain began in earnest, Buck rode into the cover of the forest and the canyon was lost from sight. Over the noise of the rain he thought he heard the sound of horses coming down the canyon.

★　★　★

Colonel Burton Russell, a large bullish man with heavy jowls and thick, grey, mutton chop side-burns, entered the upstairs conference room of Morton and Russell Land and Cattle Company at precisely 5 p.m. Punctuality was a habit acquired during his service in the War Between the States. As a young Union artillery officer, he had risen to the rank of brevet colonel due to his skill at doing the precise and complicated planning required for orchestrating the movements of artillery units. He always had his batteries where they were needed, when they were needed. At war's end, he was not at a loss of what to do with his life, like so many other veterans. He had commanded men and knew that the world held great things for Burton T. Russell.

'Gentlemen,' Russell said to the three men already in the room, 'let the meeting come to order.'

'I'm happy to tell you,' he said, once everyone was seated around the conference table, 'that we've received an offer for the Emerson Land Grant.' Russell glanced down at the telegram in his hand. 'It's from a British firm, the Marshland Company of London.' Everyone smiled at him and Russell knew what question lay in the back of each man's mind. The first to voice it was Leland Clarke, a territorial district judge, who was seated to the colonel's right.

'That's wonderful news, Burton. But are they close to what we asked?'

'Yes, very close.' Russell could see the elderly judge almost rubbing his large, bony hands together in glee, thinking about his share of $42 million. 'And,' Russell went on, 'I believe we should go over all the details of their offer. They have made a few stipulations which could be problems.'

'Such as?' The question came from the colonel's left where Anthony Brock sat. Brock, a dark, swarthy man with petulant lips, was territorial district attorney.

'First,' Russell said to him, 'a review of the details pertaining to the grant. Neddy?' Russell looked down the table at the far end where a fashionably dressed young man with dark eyes and hair sat.

'Yes, sir?' Neddy Vanders had been quietly watching the others as the colonel told them his news. But Neddy didn't wonder about the size of the offer. No, the colonel would never settle for less than he asked. As the youngest man present, Neddy was courteous to the others in the same manner a junior officer might be to his superiors. However, there was no doubt in Neddy's mind that he was intellectually superior to all present but one, the colonel, who was his mentor.

'Neddy,' Russell glanced at the telegram again and then back at Neddy, 'What is the status of the title to the grant? Is it secure yet?'

'Yes sir. We received word two days ago that Congress approved the federal surveyor's recommendation in part. Our association has been granted clear title to one hundred and eighty thousand acres. That's a fourth less than we claimed, but — '

'Why the hell didn't they go for the whole thing?' Anthony Brock interrupted loudly. 'We paid some of them stinking congressmen enough!'

'May I point out, sir, that we're lucky they didn't cut our claims a great deal more,' Neddy explained patiently to Brock, disliking the man for his crudeness and lack of finesse. 'A few associations like ours have lost all the land they claimed title to. Ours is the only one I know of that has been able to successfully increase the size of its holdings. Had it not been for the good wishes of the federal surveyor, we might only have title to the original Spanish grant of some ninety thousand acres.'

'We paid a lot of money for those so-called good wishes,' Brock snorted in contempt.

'That's correct, sir, but the costs of a few key legislators and a federal surveyor are insignificant in comparison to what we have gained.'

'Gentlemen!' Russell broke in. 'The loss of some acreage that was never really ours is not the problem. But the fact that a small tract of land within the grant boundaries belongs to someone else, is a serious matter.'

'How's that?' the judge asked. Just the idea that he might not become rich enough to retire back East, away from this god-forsaken territory, made him feel faint.

'The Marshland people want the whole area or nothing. And if Ernesto Valdez continues to refuse our offer to buy him out, we will not realize the fruits of our labours!' Russell paused to let the gravity of his remarks sink in and then continued, 'Neddy, what has been the result of our latest offer to Mr Valdez?'

'He still refuses to sell. Clay Youngblood says he knows Valdez and has agreed to pay Valdez a visit. Clay says he can persuade Valdez to change his mind.'

'You don't have to worry about Valdez anymore,' a voice interrupted. Territorial Marshal Jack Whertman strode into the room and seated himself at the conference table. 'Valdez had a fatal run-in with Clay and his boys yesterday, up in the mountains in Mora Canyon.'

'What?' Neddy didn't like being surprised. 'What happened? I saw Clay last night, over at their camp at Mora Flats. He said they was just going to talk to Valdez. Clay knew him from long ago. But Valdez got mad and started calling J.W. names and — '

'J.W.!' the colonel interrupted. 'I thought you were supposed to keep an eye on my son. That's why he was appointed as one of your deputies. Why was he with Youngblood?'

Neddy glanced at the marshal and saw his face had turned red.

'He had three days off coming to him. He said he was going to hang around home and catch up on his sleep. I didn't dream he was meeting up with Clay, honest!' Whertman looked appealingly at the rest of the men in the room and then back to the colonel.

'Finish telling about Valdez.' Neddy loathed Russell's son. The boy had his father's quick temper but lacked his father's self-control. Worse, he seemed to have inherited his mother's lack of common sense. The sooner someone did away with him the better off everyone would be.

'Clay said they rode down on Valdez and before he could get to going on him, J.W. butted in on the conversation. J.W. lost his temper and shot Valdez and also hit his daughter — '

'He killed both of them?' Neddy

interrupted. The only family Valdez had was his daughter.

'No, that's the problem.' Whertman pulled out a handkerchief and doffed his hat in order to wipe his forehead. 'J.W. only wounded Valdez. The bullet went through him and hit the girl. She was knocked off the wagon and everyone thought she was dead for sure. But Valdez got his rifle up and was going for J.W. and Clay had to shoot him. All the shooting spooked J.W.'s horse and it run off with him up the canyon. Clay and the boys gave chase but J.W. was up on that young thoroughbred mare of his and they like to never caught up with him. By the time they got J.W. straightened out and gave the horses a breather, it was two or three hours before they got back down to Valdez's wagon. All they found was a fresh grave. Clay thought it was Valdez's because he hit Valdez three or four times in the chest. But there was no sign of the girl. Clay's afraid she wasn't dead after all, and someone came along and found her.'

'Marshal, do you mean to tell me that my son was involved in a shooting and there may be a witness to it loose in these mountains?' The colonel's voice was calm, but Neddy could tell from the man's clenched fists on the table in front of him, that the colonel was furious.

'Yes, Colonel, I guess that's what it boils down to. But Clay said she was hard hit and couldn't have been taken far. He's got his boys riding the trails and ridges trying to cut sign or spot a camp.'

Whertman paused to wipe his forehead again. 'Colonel, I told J.W. to get home quick. If he was a mind to listening, he should be back in town now.'

'Thank you, Marshal.' Russell looked at Neddy. 'What do you think?'

'Marshal,' the young man said by way of reply, 'it must be understood that J.W. has not been on leave the last two days, but has, in fact, been on duty.' Neddy glanced down at the notes he had made as the marshal's story unfolded. 'Let's say he has been on duty down in La Cienega serving a warrant on someone.'

'On Julian Gutierriz for failure to appear in court,' Judge Clarke broke in.

'This can be attested to by your other deputy,' Neddy continued. 'What's his name?'

'Jake Miller.'

'Yes, Deputy Miller. He can vouch for J.W.'s whereabouts yesterday. I want to impress on you' — Neddy turned and looked at the others and then back to Whertman — 'that the veracity of the story may well stand between you and your share of forty-two million dollars!'

'Has anyone said anything about this to you?' asked Brock.

'No, not yet.'

'If they do,' Brock instructed, 'investigate it as you would any other shooting and file a full report with my office. Of course I don't think you'll find much, do you, Marshal?'

Whertman shook his head 'no'. 'Only that Clay had to shoot Valdez in self-defence and the girl was accidentally hit. His men witnessed it.'

'Gentlemen,' Colonel Russell said, 'assuming that there are no repercussions from this turn of events, what happens to Valdez's property if he is found to be without an heir? Judge Clarke?'

'Well, it's my opinion,' the old man wheezed ponderously, 'that if there were no will and no immediate kin, then the estate of the late Mr Valdez would revert to the federal government. This means that all properties included in the estate would be auctioned off.'

'Anthony?' the colonel demanded.

'In such a case, I believe we could find a front, someone to bid for us. And with forty-two million at stake I can guarantee our man would be a high bidder!'

'Thank you, gentlemen,' the colonel said. 'There's nothing else we can do until we find out the status of the Valdez girl. For now let's just plan on meeting next week at the usual time. If something comes up before then, I'll be in touch.'

As the men began to file out, Russell asked Neddy to stay. After the last man had gone, Russell pulled out two cigars and offered one to his protégé. Why, he wondered to himself, couldn't his son be more like this young man?

'What do you make of the situation, Neddy?'

'It's very likely a blessing, sir.' Neddy neatly trimmed the end off his cigar and lit it. 'Should the Valdez girl die and J.W. not be implicated, we stand to pick up the Valdez place and carry off the sale of the Emerson grant, with less trouble than if Valdez had not been shot.' Neddy puffed on his cigar and then continued, 'But should the Valdez girl live and J.W. is implicated, the good name of the Morton and Russell Land and Cattle company will be questioned and we would probably lose the sale in the end, if not more!'

'If it comes to that, we can weather it, we've weathered worse,' the colonel replied, 'and we've fairly good control of the courts and the marshal's office. I think we're safe.'

The colonel got up and walked over to look out the window. He puffed thoughtfully on his cigar and really didn't notice the people down in the square.

'I understand you are expecting a guest,' he said, turning back from the window. 'Do you have time to see that this little problem is resolved, properly?'

'I think I can manage it. My old roommate from West Point is coming but I don't expect him for several more days.'

'Good,' the colonel said, as he prepared to leave. 'Only one thing really concerns me now, and that is the person who found the Valdez girl. He's an unknown factor and therefore someone to be feared at present.'

'Don't worry, sir. I'll personally go to Youngblood's camp in the morning and ensure he takes care of both the girl and her rescuer.'

2

The sun was more than halfway across the sky when Buck heard a low moan from the lean-to behind him. He turned away from the small cooking fire and saw the girl struggling to sit up, her dark eyes wide with fright. When she saw Buck, she froze.

'Everything's all right,' he said gently, 'I'm not going to hurt you; you're safe.'

He went over to where she sat on his bedroll. She sat very still, saying nothing. Only her eyes moved, following him as he entered the lean-to and knelt down beside her to check her wound. Thinking that she hadn't understood him, Buck repeated his assurances in Spanish.

'I speak English,' she said slowly. Her voice was soft and she had only a slight Spanish accent. Then she reached up and touched her injured shoulder. The

31

effort and the touch caused her to wince from pain.

'What happened?' she asked. 'Where's my father?' She looked past Buck, out of the lean-to, and searched the camp with her eyes.

Buck didn't know what to say, or how to tell her.

'Where is he?' she demanded tearfully.

'I'm sorry, he's dead!' Buck blurted out, wishing that he could somehow soften the blow to her. She looked blankly at him for a few seconds and then the memories of Clay Youngblood and his men, and what had happened in the valley, returned.

'Oh . . . no!' she sobbed. Tears welled up in her eyes and then spilled down her cheeks as she sat looking imploringly at Buck, shaking her head from side to side, and repeating, 'No, no, no!'

Moved by the pain of her loss, and not knowing how else to comfort her, Buck awkwardly put his arms around her shoulders and held her. As she leaned against him, crying out her grief, he told her of having heard shots in the valley, of finding her father dead, and finding her, wounded, down near the creek. Lastly, he told her of burying her father.

It was almost dark when she finally stopped crying. Buck released her and went to his pack for a handkerchief. She wiped her face and blew her nose and then just sat staring down at her hands folded in her lap.

'I'm going to go check the horses,' he told her. If she heard, she gave no indication and continued to sit with her head bowed.

Buck found his horses waiting for him just outside camp. Although hobbled, they were still able to stamp and shift their weight from hoof to hoof, in the impatient manner all horses have when waiting to be fed. He slipped nosebags full of grain over their heads and stood back watching what was left of the sunset while they ate. As the brilliant orange-red western sky darkened to night, the heavens filled with a myriad of twinkling, pinpoint lights. Buck stood gazing up at the sky full of stars. He never tired of seeing the sky so lit up at night. And the night sky gave the mountains an air of tranquillity, of peace. But as he watched, he recalled a warning about these mountains from his old teacher, Major Charles Benton.

'Be careful,' the major had said, peering over a raised glass of wine. They were having dinner at the Benton home in Las Vegas, New Mexico Territory. 'Those mountains are frequented by ruffians and thieves!'

'You're not going by way of Glorieta, not taking the road to Sante Fe?' Mrs Benton glanced nervously from her husband to Buck. She was truly concerned for the safety of this young man whom she had often entertained in what she sadly recalled as far better times at a far better place than this heathen Las Vegas. She would never understand why Charles chose to retire from the Army to such a god-forsaken backwater as this.

'No, ma'am,' Buck replied, setting down his own wine glass and turning toward her. 'I plan to ride through the mountains between here and Sante Fe in order to do some hunting.'

'Clara,' Major Benton put in, 'Buck is no longer the cadet for whom you used to arrange dates.' The major suddenly smiled and chuckled. 'And remembering some of those young ladies — why, I'm surprised that Buck even visits us.'

Major Benton was right. Buck had changed. Although he stood just over six feet tall and had a lean, powerful build, it was his flashing grin and twinkling gray eyes that captured the hearts of Mrs Benton's girls. But now, at twenty-eight years of age, his once quick grin came more slowly and his eyes had lost the wonder of youth.

After graduating from West Point in 1896, Buck had spent six long years in the service of the United States Cavalry. It remained his chosen life's work even after a couple of Spanish bullets ripped through his body in the final days of the Cuban Campaign. Buck, as a regular army officer, had been assigned as an aide-de-camp to the First US Volunteer Cavalry, the Roughriders, whose second in command was a Lieutenant Colonel, by the name of Theodore Roosevelt. The colonel had been standing less than thirty yards away when the sniper's bullet struck and had rushed to the side of his fallen aide and helped drag him out of the line of fire.

Buck was sent to a field hospital and then shipped back to the States, arriving only a few weeks ahead of his unit. His recovery was hampered by a bout with pneumonia, which had left him pale and gaunt. But he had insisted on being released from the hospital in Tampa to travel to New York, where, on 13 September, Buck was present to share in that highly emotional moment when the Roughriders were mustered out of the army. There had been many red-rimmed eyes and much blowing of noses when they said farewell to

Colonel Roosevelt and to each other. It was with a touch of sadness that he said goodbye to all the volunteers he had come to know, especially one trooper by the name of Charlie McBride. It had been McBride who helped Colonel Roosevelt pull Buck out of the clearing where he lay exposed to sniper fire.

Buck was fascinated by McBride, a curious half-breed Indian several years older than Buck. McBride was a quiet, easy-going man who seemed to have taken a liking to Buck and always seemed close by, even during the fighting when Buck was up front, with the men, helping where he could. Together they had more than once risked their lives to save a fallen Roughrider.

When Buck said goodbye to McBride, the man had merely nodded and said, 'You'll be coming West soon enough. I'll be at San Carlos Pueblo when you need me.' With that, the half-breed turned and walked away.

After taking three months of convalescent leave at the family home in

Ohio, Buck reported to his next duty station, the War Department in Washington, DC. After two years of boring work, inane social functions, he met Alice: red hair, freckles, beauty and the daughter of one of the War Department's line officers, Major General Clifford B. Wilcox. Her mother, after carefully checking Buck's background and family finances, knew that he and Alice were destined for each other. And what Mother Wilcox wanted she usually got.

After a proper period of time, Buck and Alice became engaged and a wedding date was set. But the restlessness that Buck had felt ever since Cuba grew. He couldn't explain it, but he knew that something was missing in his life, something he wasn't finding in Washington, but he didn't know what. He requested a troop assignment, at any fort remote from Washington. His request was denied. He was too valuable to the War Department where he was.

Buck decided that he would take leave and go away to rethink his life. But where could he go? Then he received a letter from an old classmate from West Point, who now lived out in New Mexico Territory, in someplace called Sante Fe. Included in the letter was a standing invitation to visit should he ever get out West.

The letter brought back memories of all the stories that McBride and other Roughriders told about the West. One of their officers, convalescing with Buck in the hospital, talked about his ranch, an intriguing sounding place of wooded canyons, high mesas, and parched desert. It too, had been located in New Mexico.

'It's the most beautiful place on earth. It covers about twenty sections, that's square miles. The headquarters, a small adobe hacienda with a barn and some corrals, is located at the entrance of a hidden box canyon,' the fellow had explained to Buck. 'There are lots of trees and even a stream running through the bottom of the canyon where deer and turkey can be found all year round.'

'Sounds nice,' Buck had said.

'Nice?' the fellow had exclaimed. 'Lieutenant, it's heaven on earth. And no one knows about it because it lies between my dad's spread and the mountains. Come out to New Mexico and we'll find you a place just like it.'

The more Buck thought about it, the more he thought he would like to see this place for himself. He had once entertained thoughts of taking over his parents' farms someday, after retiring from the Army. But his parents had died and his sisters' husbands took control of the farms. So that was out. But ranching out West? And why wait for retirement? Buck went to see General Wilcox.

'I'm thinking of resigning my commission,' he told Alice's father. But General Wilcox would have none of it.

'Everyone knows you are headed for

general officer,' he told his future son-in-law, 'but Washington's War Department isn't the place for young officers like you. You need more action, more adventure and challenge. Tell you what I'll do, I'll arrange for you to take an extended leave until you get things sorted out. Then we'll find you a good posting.'

Telling Alice didn't go as smoothly. She turned pale when he told her. 'A ranch out West? Raising sheep and cows?' She could not picture herself in such a life, isolated from everyone. She thrived on carriages, balls and the social intrigues of some place like Washington, New York, or Boston. So the engagement was put on hold. Her father assured her that Buck would come to his senses.

In August of 1902, Buck loaded his horses and a few personal belongings on to a west-bound train to Las Vegas, New Mexico, where he visited his friends, the Bentons. Now, in mid-September, he was in the Sangre De Cristo Mountains, on his way to Sante

Fe. It seemed that Major Benton's warnings were going to prove prophetic.

The sound of his horses tossing their heads about so as to get to the last few grains in their nosebags brought Buck out of his reverie. He slipped off the nosebags and watched the hobbled horses clumsily make their way back out into the meadow, toward the spring at the far end. When they had disappeared into the dark, he turned and went back to camp.

The girl was up and trying awkwardly to work about the fire. She had on one of Buck's shirts from his pack. From the remnants of her blouse, she had fashioned a sling for her arm. Coffee was making and she had a skilletful of bacon frying.

'Let me do that,' Buck said as he strode into camp. 'You shouldn't be up,' he scolded, 'you need to rest and heal.' He gently guided her back under the lean-to to the bedroll and made her sit down.

'What's your name?' she asked, as

she watched him fix their supper.

'Buchanan, Buck Buchanan. And yours?'

'Emily Valdez. How long has it been since you found me?'

Buck stood up and looked at her sitting up in the lean-to. 'Four days. You ran a high fever for some time.' He knelt down to finish cooking their dinner.

'What are you doing here, in these mountains?' she asked.

'Just passing through. I'm on my way to Sante Fe, and you? Do you live around here?'

'No, about fifteen miles north of Sante Fe.'

Buck brought her a plate of food and a cup of coffee. She noticed that the food on her plate had been thoughtfully cut up into bite-sized pieces so she could easily eat with only her one good arm.

'What are you doing up here?' he asked, as he returned with his own plate and coffee. Buck sat down a few feet away and for the first time really studied her. She was very attractive, her face framed by long black hair that hung down below her shoulders. She was slender but full figured. But it was her dark eyes that caught and held his gaze when he talked to her.

'We were on our way to take supplies to one of my father's sheepherders up at the head of the canyon.'

'Did you recognize the men who shot you?'

'Yes, it was Clay Youngblood's gang that stopped us, but the man who did the shooting was J.W. Russell. He . . . his father had dealings with my father. He wanted to buy some of our land but my father wouldn't sell.'

'Do you think that's why he shot you and your father?' Buck had read about land wars in the West.

'To get our land? No, although J.W.'s father is supposed to have had several men killed or made to disappear, I don't know if that's true. He usually gets what he wants just by making life miserable for anyone who opposes him.'

'Then why did his son shoot your father?'

Emily stopped eating and, in the light of the fire, Buck could see tears coursing down her cheeks. But she fought them back and, after a few moments, slowly started eating again.

'J.W. shot my father because he didn't take J.W. seriously. Papa called him a *horniguero*, a piss-ant and laughed at him. J.W. Russell wants people to think he's as important as his father is. But the son is, how do you say, a *cobarde*, a coward who shoots old men and women . . . '

Once again Emily almost broke down but struggled to regain her composure. Her courage greatly impressed Buck, but he said nothing and they ate in silence.

'And you,' she said at last, 'tell me about Señor Buck Buchanan. Where do you come from?'

'From Ohio,' he said, and told her about the rolling green hills and farmland where he grew up, so very different from the New Mexico territory.

'And your family?' Emily wanted to know, 'a wife and children, perhaps?'

'I've been in the Army for the past several years,' Buck replied, 'and haven't had the chance to meet very many eligible ladies. So, I've remained a bachelor.' Buck wondered why he didn't say anything about Alice. Well, he rationalized, the girl hadn't asked about a fiancée.

Both fell quiet again. Buck listened to the night sounds around them, the play of the wind through the trees and the popping of small aspen sticks burning in the fire. Finally, and very gently, he asked Emily about her family.

'I have no one, now. My mother and two little brothers died in a fire four years ago. Now . . . I'm alone.'

Buck didn't know what to say. He had never been any good at making small talk with women, at least not like his friend Neddy, waiting in Sante Fe. At last she yawned.

'I think you had better lie down and rest,' he told her.

'Where do you sleep?' she asked, seeing only the one bedroll.

'Between the lean-to and the fire. A saddle blanket under me, another over me and, as we say in the cavalry, my saddle for a pillow. Not much but it's comfortable, at least to me.'

He got up, took their few dishes out to the small fire and washed them. When he looked in again, the girl was asleep on top of the bedroll. He gently pulled the blankets over her and then went out into the night.

★   ★   ★

When Emily woke, it was close to mid-morning. She went outside and found that the day was clear and the breeze coming down off the ridge above had a crisp, autumn feel to it. From the lean-to she could see the mountains to the north. Many of the aspen groves cloaking their flanks were starting to change from the summer's quaking green to autumn's shimmering gold. Emily looked for Buck but didn't see him. His rifle was missing. Perhaps he was hunting. Men! she thought.

Emily started a small fire and set coffee on to boil. She busied herself about the camp, cleaning as best she could with one arm. Her wound was still very painful. After working about the camp for a good hour she became tired and started for the lean-to. It was then that she saw them standing there, about fifty feet away, just behind the horses. There was no mistaking the tallest of the three: it was Clay Youngblood.

One of the other two men raised a rifle and aimed it at Emily. She tried to scream but no sound would come out of her mouth. So great was her fear that she stood frozen and could only stare at the death's-head grin of the man looking down the rifle at her. He knew that at fifty feet she was as good as dead, even before he pulled the trigger.

Suddenly, a small red hole appeared over his left eye. A split second later, she heard the crack of a rifle from the far side of the meadow. The outlaw dropped his rifle and was spun around by an invisible force. Emily and the other outlaws stood transfixed by the sight. She saw a red, pulpy mass where the back of his head should have been. A second later, the other outlaw beside Youngblood suddenly dropped heavily to the grass as a second shot pealed out from across the meadow.

The sound of the second shot snapped Emily out of her trance and she found herself diving into the lean-to for cover. She was vaguely aware that Youngblood had his pistol out and was shooting at her. Then she hit the ground, the impact causing white-hot pain to radiate outward from her shoulder. Emily thought she heard more shots, then the pain swept over her and she fainted.

When Emily came to, Buck was bending over her, holding a cold wet cloth to her forehead.

'Are you all right?' he asked, when he saw her eyes open. His face was grave and full of concern.

'Yes ... I think so ... Oh, my shoulder!' Emily clutched her shoulder. It felt wet. She pulled her hand away and looked at it ... it was red with blood.

'You've opened it up again,' Buck said.

He got up and went quickly to his pack and started rummaging through it for something. Emily heard him muttering but could only understand bits and pieces of what he was saying.

' ... shouldn't have gone off ... all my fault ... stupid ass ... '

'What happened to the others, those men?' She suddenly remembered the shooting.

'One got away, the tall, skinny one. I didn't think I had hit him, but I must have, because there was blood everywhere!'

'That was Clay Youngblood, the leader of the gang. But what about

50

the other two? You killed them, didn't you!'

'Yes.' Buck found what he was looking for and came over to her. Buck had several fresh bandages and started unbuttoning her shirt.

'What do you think you're doing?' she asked, as she pushed his hand away.

'I need to fix your shoulder . . . to stop the bleeding . . . I . . . I . . . ' he spluttered.

Emily saw his embarrassment and smiled inwardly to herself. 'I'm sorry, do what you have to do.'

She watched as he removed the blood-soaked bandages and cleaned her wound. As far as she could tell, he never once looked at her exposed breast. When he had finished, he slipped her shirt back up and rebuttoned it. As he worked on the last button at the top, he glanced up and saw her watching him. A wave of scarlet washed over his face.

'There,' he said hastily. 'That should do it!'

'*Gracias*,' she said softly. Her eyes caught his and held them for a moment. Then he stood.

'We're going to have to move our camp,' he said, as he looked down at her. 'The one who got away . . . what did you say his name was?'

'Youngblood, Clay Youngblood.'

'Yes, he'll probably send some of his men back up here. It would be best if we were gone by then.'

Buck bent down, scooped her up and carried her outside to a comfortable spot near the fire. While she sat and watched, he quickly struck camp and loaded the pack horse. Emily was amazed at how organized he was. It could only come from years of experience of living outside.

'Are you going to do something about those?' she asked, nodding towards the two bodies at the edge of the meadow.

'No, we'll leave them where they lie, as a warning to their friends!' He looked at the silent forms lying there.

'I've turned their horses loose but we'll take all the arms and ammunition they were carrying. We may need them.'

Emily saw a grim, hard look play across his face, and then he looked at her and his expression softened.

'We've got to get you into Santa Fe,' Buck said. 'I think you're running a fever. And we will be followed.'

Buck led his horse over to where Emily sat. He lifted her up to sit sidesaddle and then got up behind her, his arms around her to hold the reins of his big buckskin. Emily looked up at him and then, as if drawn by a magnet, she reached up and kissed him.

'For saving my life . . . and risking yours,' she said softly. Then she let her gaze fall downward and leaned back against him. She realized that she might die in the next several hours but, for the first time since losing her father, she didn't feel so much alone in the world.

3

After breaking camp, Buck had headed them into the dark forest of spruce where they were hidden from sight. Then he stopped and took out some old pieces of an army blanket and began wrapping and tying them on the horses' feet.

'Why are you doing that?' Emily had never seen anything so strange.

'These rags will help hide our tracks. All we have to do is stay on hard ground for a while. It's an old Apache trick.'

'You know the Apache?'

'No, I don't, but one of my teachers did, and he taught me.'

By midday, Buck and Emily were working through timber just below the tree-line. Their goal was a long ridge a half a mile above them. It ran north-west here, but in the distance seemed to curve ever so slowly to the west. Buck was hoping to hit a trail Emily had told him about.

As they made their way slowly through the timber, they kept hearing snatches of talking and laughter from the canyons below. A horse whinnied. Buck knew that someone was down there, patrolling and looking for them.

'Probably Youngblood's men,' he said softly to Emily.

They angled up, away from the canyons, but the timber began to thin out. Afraid of being seen from above, Buck led them downward again, several hundred feet, so they were out of sight and sound of the ridgeline above. Emily followed wearily as he guided her and the horses through the trees. It was slow going and he knew that it sapped her strength. They would go a hundred feet then run into a jumble of downed trees and have to pick their way around them. In some places trees grew too close together for them to get the horses through and they would have to change direction.

The afternoon warmed and little breeze penetrated down into the thick timber. Buck estimated that they were making less than a quarter of a mile an hour. But they hadn't made any noise and were out of sight of any of Youngblood's men. He was thankful for that.

Late in the day, they came to a narrow stream tumbling down the mountain and followed it down until it cut through a small meadow inside a stand of thick timber.

'I'm not sure where we are, but this will do for tonight,' Buck said. He began unloading the horses, and, after taking off packs and saddles, staked the horses out where they could graze.

'We're up above the Rio Maestos,' Emily told him as he worked. She smiled at him and added, 'Somewhere.'

'Do you know these mountains?' Buck had noticed the faint, teasing smile and was thankful that she could find humor in their situation. Mentally, she was holding up better than he had expected.

'I was raised in these mountains. I used to spend my summers here with my father and his flocks, before he was able to hire other shepherds. Here, let me show you.'

Emily knelt down and, in the dying light, drew a large half-circle with her finger in the dirt.

'My father used to say that these mountains make a big bowl that's open on the south.' She poked her finger into dirt at the open end of the circle, leaving a small dot in the loose soil. 'That's the village of Pecos.' Then she made a series of dots along the perimeter of the half circle. 'Six peaks rise up from the rim of the bowl and are connected by ridges that run from one peak to the next. We graze our sheep along these ridges because there are no trees there. Smaller ridges run down from the big peaks, like spokes from a wheel, toward the bowl's center where the Pecos River runs.'

Buck knelt for a better view. 'And just where are we?'

'Here,' Emily said, and made a small dot near the north-east rim of the bowl, then kept sketching with her finger as she talked.

'The Rio Maestos starts down below this ridge, called the Santa Barbara divide, and flows into the Pecos River.'

'So we have to go through the basin and over the rim on the west-side to get to Sante Fe?'

'Or take the trail that runs around the rim. It's called the Skyline trail. Sante Fe is about twenty-five or thirty miles from the top of the western rim.'

'Which way is faster,' Buck wanted to know, 'around the ridgeline or down through the basin?'

Emily thought for a minute. 'Probably around the rim, because it's above the trees and easier riding.'

'And what's it like in the basin?'

'Between the ridges that run to the center are canyons like the one you found me in. These canyons are fairly

58

open but the rest of the basin is pretty thick with timber, like here.' Emily pointed to the forest around them.

Buck kept questioning Emily until he had a mental image, a map of the mountains fixed firmly in his mind. He then sketched her drawing on a small piece of paper and put it in his pocket.

'I think I had better go up and reconnoiter the rim, in the morning.'

'Do what?' Emily was unfamiliar with the word.

'Go up to the ridgeline and look around, scout out our situation,' he explained patiently.

Emily's face paled. 'But they might see you . . . they might kill you!'

'Don't worry,' he said reassuringly, 'they won't see me, much less kill me. And I need to see if we can use the rim trails since it's the faster way.'

Emily looked flushed, as if she were feverish. Buck knew she was exhausted from the day's travel. And she wasn't able to move her left arm at all. It made him think about Otis Todd.

He had been a likeable Roughrider from Prescott, Arizona, several years older than the rest of his troop. Old Otis had been standing in front of his small tent just after his troop stopped for the night. A sniper up in some nearby palm trees shot him. Otis received a nasty shoulder wound much like Emily's.

A couple of men were detailed to get Otis back to an infirmary, while the rest of the troop flushed out and dispatched the sniper. Two days later, while carrying dispatches back to headquarters, Buck had stopped to see Otis. In the heat and dampness, the older man's wound had quickly turned bad. Otis got blood poisoning. Buck arrived just in time to see him die, quickly and painfully.

Buck was determined to get Emily to a doctor before the same thing happened to her. He feared that in a few days, a doctor would be of no use.

Camp that night was nothing more than bedrolls spread under a big

Douglas fir tree. They dared not build a fire for fear of being seen. The night air chilled Emily. She climbed into Buck's bedroll and quickly fell asleep. Buck sat in the dark listening to the night sounds of the mountains. From somewhere on the dark ridgeline to the north, a coyote barked and then started its lonely song. An owl hooted from the far side of the small meadow. Clouds rolled in, blocking out the starry sky and the air became heavy with the smell of rain. Buck put his saddle and saddle blankets next to Emily and pulled a tarp over both of them and the tack. As he was drifting into sleep, he heard the patter of raindrops on the canvas.

★ ★ ★

Buck woke just before daybreak to a light rain. He slipped quietly out of camp, leaving Emily fast asleep, and started up the mountain. By mid-morning the rain stopped and the skies cleared. He reached the top soon after, and from behind a large rock, cautiously peeked out at the trail that ran along the ridgeline. A chill swept over him as he spied two men sitting about 150 yards down the ridge to his left. He crawled back down into the timber and circled over to a small depression in the ridgeline where he could cross unseen by the two watchers.

Do it like Benton taught you, Buck told himself. Go only half as fast as you think you can go. Take your time and don't make any noise or sudden movements. You are the mountain. You are the rocks. Buck learned everything Benton could teach him in the years he was at the academy. Benton claimed that his teacher had been an old apache named Kawaykla whom he had come to know when he had been with the Apache scouts during the Geronimo campaigns.

'If I don't teach you,' Benton had told his cadets, 'you'll get yourself killed. But worse, you'll get your men killed.' Benton, for all his strange ways, had been a superb teacher and Buck had been an adept pupil.

'You would make a good Apache,' Benton told Buck at the end of his first year. 'And you would have had great fun, going south and raiding against the Mexicans.' The expression on Benton's face told Buck that the major was serious, but Buck wasn't sure if it was a compliment or not.

Now, using those same skills that Benton had taught him, Buck easily crept up to a large jumble of rocks where he could lie within earshot of the outlaws. The two men were sitting on a natural overlook that cropped out from the ridgeline. Below them spread the vast panorama of the south end of the Sangre De Cristo mountains, a huge expanse of golds, greens, deep purples and blues. From this position, the outlaws could watch all the trails leading out of the basin on its north- and east-sides. Their horses were tied out of sight, down a slope on the other side.

'Hell, they've probably gone back to Las Vegas, or over to Mora.' The speaker was a young man in his early twenties, dressed in baggy wool pants and wearing a fancy, but soiled vest. A grimy derby sat perched on his head but provided little protection from the sun. A dandy, Buck thought to himself.

'Won't do 'em any good.' The second man was equally dirty, but sensibly wearing an old broad-brimmed army hat that shaded his head and face so that only his scraggly gray beard was exposed to the sun. 'Blacky and Ramon are taking care of the trails to Mora and Las Vegas. And the way over to Sante Fe is being covered by Lee and some other boys. Clay and everybody else is riding the trails, trying to cut tracks.'

'Well, I hope we get 'em before too long.' Dandy pulled his hat off and rubbed his sunburned forehead with a dirty sleeve. 'I got to get me back down to La Cienega.'

'You just want to get back down to the cantina and that little fluff you been hanging around with lately,' Whiskered snickered. 'Better leave her alone, boy, or you'll wind up with a dose of the clap!'

Buck had heard enough. They couldn't take the quick and easy way to Sante Fe. Youngblood had them bottled up in the basin, or thought he did. Buck turned his attention from the outlaws and worked his way back down in the direction in which he had come.

* * *

Marshal Whertman left Sante Fe well before sun-up and rode eastward all day to Clay Youngblood's camp on the west-side of the mountains, at a place aptly called Horsethief Meadows. It was dark when he arrived. He saw Youngblood by the fire and called out to him, 'The colonel wants to know what's taking so long? He can't figure out why you're having so much trouble finding the Valdez girl, her being wounded and all.'

Youngblood didn't say anything; he quietly stood up from where he had been kneeling and turned to face the Marshal. The few men in camp could tell that Youngblood didn't take kindly to Whertman's remark and they began edging away from both men so as to be out of the line of fire. Whertman saw them and realized his mistake.

'Them was the colonel's words, Clay,' Whertman blurted out quickly. 'Not mine!' He cursed himself silently for being so stupid. He had forgotten how touchy Clay could be. 'Hell,' Whertman rushed on, 'I know how hard it is to find someone in these mountains if they don't want to be found. And I know you'll find the girl. I already told the colonel that.'

Youngblood remained silent and only looked at the marshal who knew that it was death itself looking at him. No one was as fast as Youngblood with a gun. And no one had less remorse in using one. But this time death passed the marshal by. Youngblood turned back to the fire, calling over his shoulder as he did so, 'Get down and get some chuck.' It was then that the marshal saw that the outlaw had been wounded. His left arm was bandaged up, just above the elbow.

Clay eased himself down on a big log that had been pulled up close to the camp's fire. 'Tell the colonel that we found the Valdez girl and the feller who took her, 'bout two days ago. The girl had been doctored and her arm was in a sling. No one else was in camp, just the girl.' Someone gave the marshal a plate full of beans and some tortillas.

'The camp was hidden good and we wouldn't have found it but for the girl. They had a pit fire built under a tree so there was no smoke or light. But she was boiling coffee and we could smell it clear down the mountain.

'We snuck up on their camp and Henry Short, you remember him, the one that came down from Colorado last year?'

Whertman had his mouth full of

beans and could only grunt and nod his head yes.

'Well, Henry drew down on the girl and was going to bust her when that son-of-a-bitch opened up with a rifle on us from the other side of the camp, off in the trees, maybe a hundred yards away. Drilled Henry right through the head. Pete Mondragon was with us and damned if he didn't get it too. I think he was hit in the chest. I opened up on the girl, but she went to cover in their tent and then I got this. But I managed to get away.

'After patching me up, all of us rode back up there but the girl and that feller were gone. They had headed into the timber and, damned me, if their tracks didn't just disappear. We buried Henry and old Pete, there in the meadow.'

Whertman finished his plate of beans and sat drinking a cup of coffee. He thought about what Clay had said.

'Sounds like this feller's got some savvy and some luck,' Whertman said. But he was thinking how he would have done it. He would have circled the camp, split up his men and come in from three sides. One man would have killed the girl while the other two backed him up. Clay had gotten careless. 'Did you get a look at him?'

'Naw, I had to drop down in the brush and crawl out of there.' Clay cradled his wounded arm. 'But he knows how to shoot and how to hide a camp. Like I said, it was just dumb luck that we stumbled across it.'

'What are you doing now? I mean, what else should I tell the colonel?'

'Tell him not to worry about the girl no more. She can't be in too good a shape and probably needs tending to by a doctor. I've got a dozen more boys coming in from Las Vegas to help cover all the trails. The rest of us will keep combing the woods for them. It's only a matter of time before we turn them up.' Clay gently massaged his wounded arm.

'This is a personal thing now!'

★ ★ ★

By sun-up Buck had the horses gathered and saddled. For the past four days they had made their way across the basin and halfway up to the pass on the west-side. Soon there would be no more suffocatingly hot stands of fir and spruce to work through, no more flies and ground bees to plague them. Today, sometime around mid-morning, they would cross over this pass and make a run for Sante Fe.

He went over to the bedrolls and woke Emily. She sat up, yawned and started to stretch her arms over her head.

'Oh!' she suddenly cried out, then looked up at Buck and smiled shyly in embarrassment. 'I forgot about the shoulder.'

'Maybe that's a sign that you're getting better.'

But he couldn't see any change. She didn't seem any worse, but he wasn't sure if she was any better. He reached down and put his hand on her forehead, studying her face for a few seconds as he did so. She felt overly warm to his touch, yet her face wasn't flushed or feverish looking.

'Do I have a fever?' she asked.

Buck's face reddened under her gaze and he quickly removed his hand.

'A little, but not much.' He didn't want to alarm her. He went to his saddle-bags and began rummaging through them. 'How about some breakfast?'

'Sí, a little . . . maybe. I'm not very hungry.'

'That's just as well.' He smiled at her, hoping to take her mind off her shoulder. 'You may not find this morning's breakfast too appetizing anyway.' He found the small bag he was looking for and brought it to Emily. 'It's pemmican, a mixture of dried berries, pounded jerky and fat, all rolled into small, bite-sized balls.'

'Don't we have any more jerky?' She was used to jerky. Her father had made it, as did almost everyone she knew. She had never eaten pemmican before.

Tentatively she nibbled at the pemmican. It had a tangy taste, probably from the berries, but she didn't like the greasy texture of it. In the end, she was able to eat only a few small bites. And she hoped she could keep even that little bit down.

★ ★ ★

By mid-morning they were resting their horses out of sight in thick timber. Just above them, a quick dash away, was timberline and above that, a narrow saddle and the pass out of the basin. On the other side was the trail down to Sante Fe. Buck told Emily to listen.

'I don't hear anything,' she said, after several minutes of silence.

'I don't either, just some crows in the distance. I think I had better go up and have look.'

Buck dismounted and helped Emily down. She sat on the ground and leaned back against a downed tree. He checked her shoulder. It was swollen and hot to his touch. The energy she had this morning had been quickly drained. Only will-power was keeping her going, now. Buck was coming to greatly respect the depth of that will-power, and her courage. He hoped she could get a few minutes' sleep while he was gone.

With their last obstacle in sight, Buck forgot his own exhaustion and worked his way quickly up the slope. Just ahead, the timber thinned and he crawled the last few yards, keeping low, until he could get a clear look at the saddle. He couldn't see anyone, but he sensed someone was there.

He studied the saddle and how the trees grew up the slopes of the peaks on either side. Then he saw it, a thin ribbon of smoke rising up through the trees a couple of hundred yards to the right of the saddle. A camp! And someone would be sitting in the edge of the timber up there, watching.

For several minutes Buck lay there, concentrating. They needed a diversion, but how? Then he remembered a story that Major Benton had told. He and his scouts had waited in ambush in the mountains above Fort Bowie, down in Arizona. Buck smiled to himself as he remembered Benton telling how a small band of Apache raiders made fools of him and his men.

★ ★ ★

He found Emily asleep sitting up. Buck shook her gently to wake her.

'Youngblood's men are guarding the pass.' He saw a look of despair sweep across her face. He smiled at her. 'But I have a plan to pull them away from the pass until we're through it.' He explained what he had in mind.

'Will it work?' she asked. The despair had vanished.

'It worked once before, a long time ago.' He studied her thoughtfully, wondering if she was up to what he was going to ask of her. 'But I need your help. Think you're up to it?'

'*Sí*! I can help!' She struggled to her feet.

'Take the horses and lead them forward, up the slope, until you see the timber thinning. Stay there, out of sight, until I join you.'

Buck searched through his saddle-bags until he found a box of rifle cartridges and some matches. He put a handful of both into his pocket.

'See you in a little while.' He smiled reassuringly at her and then disappeared into the timber.

The timber was thick but without the horses Buck slipped quickly through it and made his way up to the left of the saddle, on the opposite side from Youngblood's men. He stopped when he was level with them and he was about 300 yards back in the timber. Buck found a small clearing and piled up firewood as if he were making two large camp-fires. In the center of each pile, he placed half of the rifle cartridges and then began laying a trail of kindling down slope from each pile of wood. When he had a line of kindling piled up about four feet long to one fire and another six feet long to the second, he set fire to both trails of kindling.

'I hope this works,' he muttered to himself as he scrambled back down to meet Emily. She had led the horses to within fifty yards of timberline and had kept them out of sight in a thick grove of limber pine.

'When the bullets go off and those men up there ride into the timber on the other side, I want you to go ahead of me. Ride hard over the saddle,' Buck told her. 'Don't look back and don't stop for anything. I'll be behind you a ways and will catch up on the other side.'

'But what if something happens to you?' She was scared. He could see it in her face and hear it in her voice.

'Don't worry,' he said as reassuringly as he could. 'Nothing is going to happen to me. But you keep riding and don't stop until I catch up with you, or you get to Sante Fe!'

Before he could say anything more, a

tremendous volley of shots came from the trees on the left of the saddle. From up on the right of the saddle came shouting and then Buck saw five horsemen riding hard across the open part and into the timber on the side where the shots came from. As the riders dismounted at the edge of the trees, there was a second volley of shots. The outlaws quickly disappeared into the forest.

'Now!' he told Emily and whacked her horse on the rump.

She sped up toward the pass, her horse at a dead run. Buck was several feet behind her and saw her lean down low over the neck of her horse. She knew how to ride and it would take an exceptional rider on a fast horse to overtake her. But as they neared the top, something moving on the right and lower down the slope caught his eye. Two riders were coming at an angle from the outlaws' camp. He wondered if they had been laggards or asleep when his diversion went off. It didn't matter because they were here now, coming hard. He didn't understand why they didn't stop and fire. If they tried to catch him and Emily, he could take care of them and not alert the rest of the men in the trees. If they started shooting, he and Emily would lose the headstart for Sante Fe that they so desperately needed.

Then Emily was up and over the saddle. Buck, close behind, raced Alamo over the crest and then brought the big horse around, out of sight of their pursuers. But he could hear them coming hard. Buck reached back and pulled out his saber. The loud rasping sound of the three-foot blade slithering out of its scabbard always made the hair on Buck's neck raise up.

From the sounds of their horses, Buck guessed that the two riders were about twenty yards below the crest. He put his spurs to Alamo and charged back over. It was a classic cavalry charge. The two outlaws were less than five yards below him, riding close together, one slightly in front of the other. Buck's saber slashed down and across the first outlaw as he passed close by. Then Alamo crashed down on the second rider's horse, knocking it down and unseating its startled rider. The man scrambled to his feet as Buck wheeled Alamo around and charged down on him again. Buck's saber swept down just as the outlaw was raising his pistol.

Buck stopped momentarily, and glanced downslope towards the timberline but he saw no one. He turned and once more rode hard over the crest and down the trail leading to Sante Fe.

4

It was early evening when Buck and Emily rode into Sante Fe. Smoke from cook stoves lay heavily over the huddle of squat adobe houses on the outskirts of town. Only a few people were out and about, but he sensed that many of the town's inhabitants watched out of darkened doorways as he and Emily rode past. She led the way, hunched over in her saddle and swaying from fatigue or her wound, or both. Buck couldn't tell.

She led them to a large, flat-roofed house surrounded by a high adobe fence. She stopped her horse in front of a large, solid wooden gate in the fence and just sat, bent over with exhaustion.

'Where are we?' Buck asked.

'This is the home of my father's best friend, Victorio Lucero.' She didn't look up. 'We'll be safe here.'

Buck got down from his horse and knocked on the big gate.

'Hello in the house!' he shouted, '*Hola en la casa!*'

A middle-aged Mexican opened the gate. He started to say something, but looked past Buck and his eyes went wide with surprise. Buck turned to follow his gaze. Emily had fallen from her horse and lay unmoving. Both men ran to her and Buck lifted her from the ground.

'Quick,' said the man, 'bring her this way!' He led them through the gate and into the house. 'Emilio,' he said to a young boy who opened the door to the house for them, '*vaya para el doctor!*'

Buck was led down a wide hallway with windows looking out on to a patio. The man ushered him into a large, whitewashed bedroom. An older woman and two teenage girls followed them in. Buck gently laid Emily on the bed. She was pale and her breathing shallow.

'Come, *señor*,' the man said, taking

Buck by the arm and guiding him toward the bedroom door. 'My wife and daughters will care for her now.'

Outside Emily's room, the man turned and held his hand out to Buck. 'My name is Victorio Lucero. I am a close friend of the Valdez family. I have sent for the doctor. While we wait for him, we can tend to your horses.'

Buck and Lucero had finished their chores and were waiting in the living-room when the doctor arrived. He was an older man with the worn look of someone who never gets enough sleep. Buck briefly told him what happened and about Emily's wound. Then one of Lucero's children led the doctor away to Emily's room.

'She's very lucky that you came along when you did,' Lucero said as they waited. 'We feared the worst for her. One of her father's men found their wagon and dead horse. He and the other sheepherders searched for them but, of course, to no avail. And Youngblood's ruffians were riding the trails, too.' Lucero paused and then asked politely, 'What lucky circumstances brought you to be in the Sangre de Cristos?'

Buck explained his hunting trip and coming to Sante Fe to see an old friend.

'What is your friend's name? I'm sure I must know him.' Lucero laughed, 'Sante Fe is such a small town that everyone knows each other. I will send word that you are here.'

'His name is Neddy Vanders.'

A look of surprise came to Lucero's face. 'Yes, I know him.' The warmth and friendliness that had been in Lucero's voice was suddenly gone. 'How is it you became friends?'

Buck explained about West Point and rooming with Vanders. Lucero studied Buck intently as he spoke.

'How long has it been since you last saw your friend?'

'About six years, and then only briefly in Washington. Why?' Lucero's coldness and his prying questions were becoming annoying. 'What are you getting at?' Buck asked sharply.

'I'm sorry,' Lucero said. His voice sounded a little friendlier. 'I've had dealings with Vanders, in the past, as have many of our friends.'

Buck sensed that Lucero, for whatever reason, did not like or approve of Neddy Vanders. But before he could ask Lucero, the doctor returned from caring for Emily.

'I think she'll be all right,' he told Lucero, 'if we can stop what infection is in her wound from spreading. And she needs to get plenty of rest and quiet so as to regain her strength.' Then the doctor turned to Buck.

'It's a good thing you got her here when you did, young man. Another day or two and the infection would have spread so far that she would have needed a priest instead of a doctor.' He started for the door then turned back to Buck. 'You did a very professional job of patching up her shoulder. It's obvious that you've had a good deal of experience in such matters.'

Buck was aware of Lucero watching him, waiting for his reply. Lucero had not yet made up his mind about Buck and it had something to do with Buck and Neddy's friendship.

'I was in the Army and helped care for several wounded men during the Cuban campaign.' Buck felt uncomfortable talking about himself and changed the subject. 'But there's now the matter of reporting the murder of Emily's father and the attack on us to the local authorities.'

Lucero and the doctor exchanged glances. The doctor started to say something, then seemed to think better of it and left.

★ ★ ★

Fifteen minutes later, Buck was in the marshal's office on the south-east corner of the town plaza. 'Let me get this straight,' Marshal Whertman said after listening to Buck's story, 'you claim that Clay Youngblood and his men killed Juan Valdez and tried to kill his daughter?'

'Miss Valdez said that the person who actually shot her and her father was someone named Russell.' Buck disliked the lawman. No chairs had been offered and Buck had been left standing in front of the marshal's desk while Buck told what happened. It was an old trick that officers often used to intimidate subordinates. But Buck wasn't going to be intimidated.

'Just what were you doing up there in those mountains?' Whertman asked.

'I was on my way to Sante Fe, from Las Vegas.'

'You were a long way from the road between here and Las Vegas.'

'I was relaxing, doing a little hunting and enjoying the scenery.'

'Funny way to relax,' Whertman snorted. 'Well, I'll make a report of what you told me and get back to you on it.'

'That's all?' Buck knew he had just been dismissed and felt his face flush with rising anger. 'A man's been murdered, his daughter shot and all you're going to do is make a report?'

Whertman leaned forward over the desk, toward Buck. 'Listen,' he said, 'I think you have your story wrong. I have witnesses that say it was self-defense. They say that Valdez drew down on Youngblood. The girl just got caught in the crossfire.'

'She says it was Russell who shot her, not Youngblood.'

'Well,' Whertman said, 'it couldn't have been J.W. because he was in another part of the country, with two other deputies, serving a warrant. I'm afraid the Valdez girl is just feeding you a line, trying to start something.' Whertman stood up as if to finally bring the conversation to an end. But Buck didn't budge.

'Why would she do that?'

'Now how-in-hell do I know what's going on in her head or why she's lying! Russell's old man's rich and maybe she was going to try and get some money from him. Anyway, I've at least six people who say she's lying.'

'And me? What about me, Marshal, am I lying too?' Buck's voice had changed, had become soft, controlled and full of menace. 'Those men tried to kill Miss Valdez at my camp later. I had to defend her. Two of them were killed. Did your witnesses say anything about that, or how Youngblood's men patrolled all the trails in order to prevent us from coming to Sante Fe? Did your witnesses say anything about that?'

Whertman was losing his patience. Just who did this travel-worn and dirty stranger think he was. 'Mr Buchanan, you didn't see the shooting and I have several men who did. It's their word against the girl's. As for you killing somebody, I'm going to look into that also, so don't leave town. Where can I find you?'

'I don't know.' Buck knew from years of having to deal with stupid and vindictive superiors that there was no use in arguing further with the marshal.

'I guess at the local hotel. I'm here to visit a friend, Mr Neddy Vanders.'

At the mention of Vanders, the Marshal's attitude suddenly changed.

'Mr Buchanan, I promise you there will be a thorough investigation and I'll report back to you. Perhaps the Valdez girl was just rattled by the shooting and being hurt. Her father had a reputation for a quick temper. Who knows? But I'll find out and get back to you.'

The marshal escorted Buck and Lucero out of his office and on to the walk outside.

'Since you're a friend of Neddy Vanders,' Whertman said softly so that only Buck could hear, 'let me give you some advice. That girl you helped, the Luceros and all that bunch . . . well, they're troublemakers and sworn enemies of your friend. They can't be trusted. But don't just take my word for it, go ask Vanders.'

* * *

Whertman closed the door behind Buck and went back to his desk. He sat thinking of all the things that he had been through since leaving Missouri. He didn't want anything or anyone to mess things up for him now. Life was nice in Sante Fe. And, at 57 he was too old to start over somewhere else. Buchanan and the girl could raise a big stink and, too, Buchanan might have connections and could ruin things for Whertman, the colonel and even that snooty Vanders. But Buchanan could be taken care of, Vander's friend or not. Besides, in the end it would be for Vander's good too.

'Snyder!' Whertman yelled to his deputy dozing on a bunk in one of the cells in back. 'Get your lazy butt out here.'

Several minutes passed and finally a man stumbled through the door from the cellblock.

'Yeah?' He rubbed sleep from his eyes.

'Run down to Juanita's place and see

if Clay got in yet. If he's there, tell him the Valdez girl and the guy who killed his men are in town. Tell him the guy's name is Buchanan, Buck Buchanan and he's staying at the hotel. The girl's over with the Lucero bunch.'

Snyder jammed on his hat and started for the door.

'Just a minute,' Whertman said. 'Tell Clay I'll be out of town from now until late tomorrow night. And so will you deputies. We got to all go over to the other side of Lamy and check out a report of rustling.'

★　★　★

Sante Fe's only hotel was located on the town plaza. Like most of the other buildings in town, it was a low adobe structure with a tin roof. Inside was a lobby and dining hall in the front, and two long wings of rooms extending back from the plaza. The rooms were well furnished and comfortable, but after being outside for so many weeks,

91

Buck felt hemmed in. He had no clean clothes. Those were cached up in the mountains. Still, he washed and cleaned up as best he could. Then he went to find something to eat.

The dining hall was closed for the evening, but the waitress, an older, grandmotherly woman, let Buck in and fixed him a sandwich. While he was eating the desk clerk came in with a message. It was from Neddy's wife. The note said Neddy was out of town but was due to return the next day. Included was a dinner invitation for the evening of Neddy's return. The note ended by saying they had a big surprise for Buck.

Before Buck went to bed he decided to take a walk. Without intending to, he found himself heading toward Lucero's. In the back of his mind was the thought of checking on Emily. The evening was cool. Pungent, sweet smoke from fireplaces filled the night air. Only the plaza was lit by the dim glow of a few street lamps. The rest of the town was dark and he had to pick his way carefully along the narrow streets.

About halfway to Lucero's Buck started feeling that something or someone was following him. He looked back but could see nothing but the dark shadows of walls and fences. Yet the feeling stayed with him as he walked. He slowly eased his service revolver out of its holster and held it low against his leg so as not to be noticeable. Buck reached the Lucero house and pounded on the gate. He heard someone come out and then a voice asked who was there.

'Buck Buchanan. I wanted to see how Miss Valdez is.'

He heard an iron bar being slid back from the gate and then it opened. Just as Buck started in, he heard the action of a rifle being worked in the darkness behind. He dove to the ground as two shots rang out. Plaster chips showered him as slugs tore into the adobe fence just above his head. Buck had his revolver up and thumbed off two quick shots at the point in the dark where he had seen the muzzle blasts. Rapidly, he rolled to his left several feet as one more shot rang out and a slug plowed up the ground where he had lain. Shouts came from the house and Buck heard someone running back down the street.

'Señor Buchanan! Señor Buchanan!' It was Lucero.

'I'm all right!' Buck called.

Lucero and his sons came out of the gate. They had a lamp that lit up the street. He and his sons all carried rifles. One of the younger Luceros saw something near the neighbor's water trough. He called to his father and Lucero went over with the light.

'*Ai, Dios!*' Lucero called out in surprise. Buck joined them. A man lay face down in the dirt. Lucero rolled him over on his back and held up the lantern.

'You know him?' Lucero asked.

Part of the dead man's bearded face was covered with blood from a bullet hole just under his eye. But Buck could still recognize him. It was the man from the ridgeline, the one Buck had nicknamed 'Whiskers'.

Lucero then ushered Buck into the house.

'What happened?' Lucero asked, as he filled two glasses generously with dark, red wine. Keeping one, he handed the other to Buck and said, 'Tell me everything that happened, from the time you left here.'

* * *

Emily was asleep when Buck stopped by Lucero's the next day. He needed clothes to wear to dinner that night so he walked around the town plaza and down some of the side streets where stores and mercantiles were located. Buck was surprised at the number of Indians in town, many buying supplies or just lounging around.

The afternoon was almost gone when Buck returned to Lucero's. Emily was now awake and he was ushered into her room. One of Lucero's daughters sat discreetly in one corner. Emily had lost most of her pallor and Buck once more found himself admiring her natural beauty. Alice always wore lots of make-up and perfume. Buck didn't think he had ever seen her without some on. But Emily presented herself just as she was, with no pretenses. Buck liked that.

'Oh Buck,' she said, taking his hand, 'Señor Lucero told me about the ambush! And all because of me!'

'Well, that may be, but there's more to it than that, at least now.' Buck told her of his visit with the marshal.

'The marshal refused to do anything about your father's murder! He said it was self defense, that your father was about to shoot J.W.' Buck didn't like what he was about to say but he had to be sure all the shooting and the shock of being hit hadn't confused Emily. 'Is that how it happened?'

Emily withdrew her hand from

Buck's and looked hard at him.

'Buck, I told you what happened. My father did have his rifle across his lap, but he wasn't holding it when J.W. shot him.' She looked imploringly at Buck.

'You believe me, don't you?'

'Yes, yes,' Buck reassured her and took her hand in his again. 'It's just that the marshal claims he has witnesses, who swear that J.W. wasn't even there and that Youngblood shot your father in self defense. It's your word against theirs.'

'How, then, does this marshal explain J.W. shooting me?'

'He says you were accidentally hit in the exchange of fire between your father and Youngblood,' Buck told her.

She looked up at Buck, her face flushed with anger. 'Maybe I was hit accidentally, but it was J.W. who shot my father in cold blood. All this really means is that the marshal will do nothing!'

'It seems that way.' Buck could understand her anger. He was angered by it himself. 'I also told him about the men who attacked our camp and tried to stop us in the pass. It didn't seem to matter one bit to him. He just said he would look into it and let me know what he found out.'

'Everyone in Sante Fe knows that the marshal is in with Youngblood and several others here, including Burton Russell,' Emily said, her blaze of anger subsiding. 'These people are stealing land and selling it as their own. My father told me about it.'

'That would explain the marshal and his deputies being conveniently out of town last night when I was ambushed.'

For a long time Emily sat holding Buck's hand and staring out the court-yard window. Finally, she shrugged her shoulders and sighed deeply.

'Nothing will be done,' she said, fighting back tears. 'My father's killer will go free.'

'Perhaps not,' Buck said, hoping to cheer her up. 'I plan to wire the Justice Department in Washington, D.C. A friend of mine is high up there and can help get an investigation into all this, since this is Federal territory.'

'How long will that take?' Emily muttered, seemingly unimpressed with Buck's plan.

'I don't know. I'll send my wire tomorrow.' Buck paused, thinking about it. 'We should hear back within a week or two, if my friend is in Washington.

'And when will the killer of my father be punished?'

'That may take a few months — '

'Or years,' she interrupted hotly. 'Or never! Yes, more likely never! Oh, I wish I were a son instead of a daughter. I would bring J.W. to justice!'

'You mean shoot it out with him?' Buck was shocked. 'Just like in the old days?'

'If I were a man like you, yes, that is what I would do!'

'Is that what you want me to do?' But Buck knew what her answer was going to be, even as he asked.

'You are a man . . . ' Emily's

demeanor turned from anger to ice cold.

'But I'm no pulp magazine hero,' Buck retorted, annoyed with her for what she was now asking him to do. 'I'm no gunfighter. We'll let the law take care of this. If the marshal won't do it, the Department of Justice will. After all, this is 1902; times have changed.'

'Maybe where you come from,' she argued back, 'but this is New Mexico territory, not some fine Eastern city!'

Buck stayed with her for a while longer but she was noticeably cold and would not talk to him. He suspected that she was brooding on her father's death and J.W. On his way out Buck told Lucero what had happened.

'She may be right,' Lucero replied, 'and justice will be served no other way.'

'My God, man!' Buck said in disbelief, and he heard himself repeating what he told Emily. 'This is 1902, doesn't anyone out here know that times have changed?'

* ★ ★

At six that evening, a servant with a carriage called for Buck at his hotel and took him to the Vanders'. Neddy met him at the door. His joy in seeing Buck was apparent. But Lucero was right, Neddy had changed. Gone was the hesitant, fresh-scrubbed and innocent-looking young cadet who had once shared four years of Buck's life. Experience had tempered Neddy and he now had a way about him that bespoke of power and great self-assurance.

'You don't know how pleased I am that you've finally come to Sante Fe,' Neddy said smoothly, as he escorted Buck into the house. 'However, I can't say I am too pleased with the company you've fallen in with and must warn you about them. We'll talk about that later. Right now, I have a great surprise for you!'

Neddy led Buck into a spacious parlor where three ladies were sitting waiting. One placed where Buck could see her as he entered, was a striking blonde whom Buck took to be Neddy's wife. The others had their backs to the door.

'Ladies, may I present Captain Buck Buchanan,' Neddy announced grandly.

The other two women rose and turned toward Buck. Neddy was right: Buck was greatly surprised. It was Alice and Mother Wilcox.

'Alice,' Buck blurted out, 'what in God's name are you doing here?'

Alice turned pale. Mother Wilcox visibly winced at Buck's words, as though she had been slapped. She puckered up her mouth in distaste.

'I mean, this really is a surprise,' Buck stammered quickly, trying to cover up his lapse of manners. ' . . . A pleasant surprise I mean . . . '

Both mother and daughter seemed transfixed by Buck's outburst. It was Neddy's wife who took charge and smoothed things over.

'So, you're the famous Buck Buchanan.' Her voice was soft and teasing, but she had the same air of self-assurance as Neddy. 'My husband has told me all about your exploits at the academy.'

'Buck,' Neddy said, as he went to his wife's side, 'may I present Vivian Vanders, my wife.'

Buck couldn't help thinking that Neddy had done well for himself, judging from the fine house, servants and beautiful wife. Neddy had left the army shortly after graduation from the academy and had gone to seek his fortune.

Alice recovered from her shock, and rushed over to Buck. He bent over to kiss her hello. After the cool, clean air of the mountains, her perfume was overpowering. Buck wondered what she really smelled like.

'I have been able to obtain a key to a certain room at the hotel,' she whispered softly. 'And I'll be over as soon as Mother falls asleep.' She smiled covetously at Buck.

Alice looked very desirable. Her evening gown showed off her full figure to every advantage. And Buck remembered how lustful Major General Wilcox's little girl could be.

Dinner was served and Buck enjoyed the mild teasing of Neddy's wife. Mother Wilcox, on the other hand, sat with her lips pursed in disapproval of most things, the food, the talk, and most of all, Buck.

He told them about finding Emily Valdez and their flight through the mountains from Youngblood's gang. Alice and Vivian were full of comments about how terrible his ordeal must have been. But Neddy said very little. He listened and watched Buck as the story unfolded.

Following dinner, the two men retired to Vander's drawing-room while the women went to freshen up.

'I've heard several stories about your trip through the mountains with Miss Valdez,' Neddy said as he offered cigars, 'and they differ somewhat from yours.'

Neddy lit his cigar and looked at Buck. 'What really happened?'

'Just what I said at dinner.'

'Tell me again,' Neddy insisted, 'and don't spare me the gore.' So Buck retold his story to Neddy, leaving out nothing. Again his friend just listened. After Buck had finished his story, Neddy sat in silence for several seconds, going over what his old roommate had told him.

'Is it your opinion that Marshal Whertman discounts your version?' Neddy finally said.

'Yes, for some reason.' Buck thought a moment. 'I suspect he may be tied in with Youngblood, somehow. At least that is what Victorio Lucero seems to think.'

'Buck, you must learn to take what the local people say with a grain of salt.' Neddy leaned forward to emphasize his points. 'They are a simple people and know nothing of our ways. Consequently, many feel unscrupulous Americans have duped them out of their businesses or lands. So, naturally they resent us.'

'Was someone trying to dupe Emily's father out of his lands?' Buck wanted to know.

'No, that's not the case at all.' Neddy paused for a few seconds as if trying to decide on something. 'I am personally involved in the attempted purchase of Valdez's lands. No one has tried to force him off his land. He was offered many times more than what it was worth. In fact, he could have bought another place three or four times larger than his present holding.'

'Are you,' Buck asked coldly, 'also involved with Youngblood and his gang?'

'Youngblood works for the Land and Cattle Association of which I'm a member. He oversees the care of our herds. Perhaps I should explain what has been happening.'

Neddy smoothly started outlining the dealings of the land and cattle association he worked for. He did, however, omit the names and titles of various members, referring to them only as investors. Then he told Buck about the Emerson Land Grant and how Valdez's property was a key piece in the Grant's sale.

'And you say that all this is legal?' Buck asked, when Neddy was through.

'Yes, or I wouldn't be a part of it.' Neddy sat puffing his cigar. 'We've driven some hard bargains in the past, but we have always been fair and honest about them. And we don't kill people to get their land. If Valdez wouldn't sell, we would have put the deal together some other way, without his land.'

Buck couldn't help thinking that his friend had changed greatly since leaving West Point. He had become smooth and polished. Glib, some would have called him. But Major Benton, in his characteristic bluntness, would have called Neddy slippery. And Buck had the feeling that there were a lot more details that Neddy had conveniently left out.

'There are several things I don't

understand,' Buck said. 'I don't understand Youngblood's attack on my camp and why the marshal won't investigate this whole thing.'

'The first is easy to explain,' Neddy laughed. 'Youngblood thought you were one of the outlaws who have taken to the mountains to avoid the law. He has been shot at several times up there. This may be the same thing that Whertman thought. And, too, Valdez had a reputation as a headstrong man that often quarreled with Americans. I know that he personally disliked J.W. and picked several fights with him.'

'I see,' Buck said, 'that would explain some things.' Buck showed no emotion, but inwardly he was shaken at how glib his old roommate had become. And he found it hard to believe that Neddy thought Buck would be satisfied with such simple-minded explanations.

'And, as for your second point, I can guarantee that Whertman will make a full investigation,' Neddy added.

'I told Whertman that I expected

such. I do have friends in the Justice Department in Washington.'

'No need for that,' Neddy said smoothly. 'But now, let's discuss something more pleasant. I've been authorized to offer you a part in our land and cattle company. I personally would like to have you for a partner. We can meet tomorrow and I can convince you that we are law-abiding businessmen. There is even opportunity for newcomers.'

'I'm flattered that you still regard our friendship so highly . . . I don't know what to say.' Buck thought for a bit. 'I appreciate your offer, but until this Valdez business is cleared up, I can't really make such a decision.'

Buck was suddenly interrupted by Vivian Vanders, who rushed into the room.

'A messenger just came from the marshal . . . Oh God! It's terrible! J.W. was just shot and killed . . . down at Webster's!'

Neddy stubbed out his cigar and sprang to his feet.

'What happened? Do they know who did it?' he demanded.

'Yes,' his wife said. Then she looked at Buck. 'It was that Valdez girl. They've got her in jail right now.'

5

A crowd had already formed outside the jail by the time Buck and Neddy arrived. Fear of a lynch mob raced through Buck until he saw Lucero and several other Mexicans in the crowd. Buck decided that many were there out of curiosity. But, like Lucero, a significant number were there because they were friends of Emily or her father.

'They won't let anyone see her!' Lucero told Buck. 'We're worried if she is all right. She's still weak and may need a doctor.' Lucero's gaze bore into Neddy. 'And that piss-ant marshal of yours won't call one.' Lucero's concern was evident and so was the large Colt revolver strapped to his waist.

'We'll get in,' Neddy assured Lucero and the other Mexicans who crowded around them. 'Then Captain Buchanan can vouch for her condition and, if a doctor is required, he will be summoned immediately.'

Neddy turned and headed for the jailhouse door. But Lucero pulled Buck back momentarily.

'They've got Emily where they can take care of her now, and get her land,' Lucero said in a low voice. 'Watch yourself, or they'll get you too.'

Buck caught up with Neddy and followed him through the jailhouse door, which had been opened to them. Inside were Marshal Whertman and three deputies.

'What happened, Marshal?' Neddy asked.

'J.W. and these boys here were down at Webster's shooting pool when the Valdez girl shows up with this old horse revolver. The boys tried to take it away from her, but before they could she shot J.W. in the belly. Doc Simmons came and worked on him but the boy died.'

He's lying, Buck told himself. The story sounds rehearsed and he didn't believe Emily capable of just walking in and shooting anybody.

'Are you sure that's what happened?' Buck demanded hotly.

'My deputies were both there, Buchanan.'

'I want to see her,' Buck said, 'and hear her side of it.'

'Well, I don't know,' Whertman said peevishly. 'Judge Clarke said not to let anyone in. We don't want anyone to spring her or lynch her.' Whertman grinned maliciously at Buck. 'You wouldn't do any of those things, would you?'

'Certainly not!' Buck could feel his anger building.

'Good,' the marshal smirked, ''Cause we want her here to stand trial for killing J.W. Judge Clarke's gonna try her the day after tomorrow.'

'That's enough, Marshal!' Neddy said sharply. The smirk vanished. 'Captain Buchanan can see her anytime he wants to, do you understand?'

'Yes,' the marshal muttered, like a

chastened playground bully.

'Now, what's this about a trial?' Neddy gave the marshal his full attention. 'What did Judge Clarke say?'

'Just to make sure that no one got her out 'cause he was going to see that she gets a speedy trial.' Whertman glanced at Buck and then continued, 'Brock was with him and talked to these boys.' Whertman nodded toward his deputies.

'Brock is a territorial district attorney,' Neddy explained to Buck. 'Go on, Marshal.'

'That's about it. Except Brock said it looked like a simple case of cold-blooded murder and we should start building the hanging gallows right away.' Whertman looked at Buck and once more gave him a nasty smirk.

But instead of letting his anger get the better of him, Buck took a deep breath and let it out slowly. He knew what was coming. Sooner or later, just like at West Point, when an upper-classman took an overzealous delight in hazing you, there came a time when it was just you and him. Neddy may have been noted for his uncanny ability to focus on issues, but Buck had been known for his patience. Sooner or later, it would be just him and Whertman!

*　*　*

Buck and Neddy were taken to the cell block behind the marshal's office. Emily was lying unconscious on a cot in the last cell. She was handcuffed and her legs were shackled. A short chain ran from her shackles to the wall on the cell.

'Get these chains off her,' Neddy said angrily, as he noted the shocked look on Buck's face. 'In fact, take off the handcuffs and shackles! She's not going to escape.'

'These are just standard for murderers,' Whertman grumbled, as he freed the unconscious girl.

'And why hasn't the doctor been summoned?' Neddy demanded.

'We tried to get him but he was out,'

Whertman said.

'Well, try and get him again . . . now! In fact, go yourself, but see that he gets here as soon as possible!'

After the marshal had gone, Neddy turned to Buck, giving him his full attention.

'I apologize for this treatment of Miss Valdez,' Neddy said. 'We are not savages and have nothing against this girl.' But even with all of his attention focused on Buck, Neddy was unable to tell what Buck was thinking. From years of army service, dealing with sadistic upper-classmen and loutish superiors, Buck had learned how to become completely impassive so no one would know what he was thinking.

Neddy left to go to his employer's house. Buck sat down on the edge of Emily's cot to await the doctor. One of Whertman's deputies sat on a bench outside the cell. Emily felt feverish again and Buck's old fear of infection returned. Finally the doctor came.

'She's pretty weak,' he said, after

examining her. 'It must have taken all her strength to go down to Webster's and confront that gang. Anyway, she seems more exhausted than anything else. Unfortunately, I don't think she'll get much rest in here.'

The doctor gave Buck some medicine and then left. As the night slowly passed, Buck sat with Emily, watching her and thinking about all they had been through. She was so different from Alice or Neddy's wife. Emily was alone and vulnerable. Did she, he wondered, really shoot J.W.? She was capable of doing so. But, he reminded himself, only if her life were threatened.

As dawn broke, Emily stirred and tried to sit up. She looked around, confused, then saw Buck. She threw her arms around him and started crying.

'Oh, Buck,' she sobbed, 'tell me it's all a bad dream, tell me I'm not here, in this jail!'

Buck held her tightly. 'It will be all right,' he said softly.

He could feel Emily relax and her crying subside.

'Can you tell me what happened?' he asked gently.

'I couldn't just sit and do nothing while my father's killer went free.' Emily began to cry again. 'I went to Señor Lucero's study but he was not in. The whole family had gone to church for prayers. I saw a gun, a *pistola*, on the desk. The more I looked at it, the more I wanted to bring J.W. to justice, to make him confess to shooting me and killing my father.'

'Then what did you do?' Buck wiped away her tears with his shirt sleeve.

'I went out to find J.W. He was easy to find. Everyone in town knows that he and his friends are always at Webster's. He was there last night, drinking and playing pool.' Emily took a deep breath and then continued.

'I confronted him and told him he wasn't going to get away with shooting me, with killing my father. He just laughed at me.'

'Did you point your gun at him or threaten him with it?'

'No, it was in my coat pocket. I didn't take it out until he said he was going to have some fun with me and then finish what he started. I was suddenly so afraid. It was like cold water hitting me in the face and waking me up. Why did I think I could go in there by myself and not be harmed,' Emily took a deep breath then went on.

'I pulled the *pistola* out, cocked it and pointed it at J.W. I told him he had better leave me alone, but he just laughed at me and took my gun away. I just let him do it. He knew I wouldn't really shoot him, and that I was just bluffing. Someone grabbed me from behind and threw me down on the floor, next to the pool table. I was petrified with fear then, because I knew what he meant to do to me. As he unbuckled his belt, he tossed Señor Lucero's *pistola* down on the pool table and it went off. He looked so surprised, then doubled over and fell to the floor.

Everybody started yelling. People grabbed me and held me until the marshal came and I was arrested.'

'Then you didn't shoot him, he shot himself,' Buck told her. 'The trial should be a mere formality.'

'But all the witnesses are his friends,' Emily sobbed. 'They won't tell the truth. And they will hang me and get my father's ranch!'

★　★　★

Just as Whertman had said, Emily's trial was held two days later. The courtroom was located on the second floor above the marshal's office and jail. The room was large and open with lots of benches for spectators. Still, Buck was glad he got there early because the courtroom filled up quickly. Lucero came in and sat next to him.

'Sante Fe's finest.' Lucero said sarcastically and pointed at the spectators.

Most looked like ruffians or drifters. But Buck was also surprised at the number of Indians in the courtroom.

'They attend every trial, but no one knows why, for sure,' Lucero told him. 'Perhaps they want to see how the white-man's justice works, or maybe they are just bored and are seeking entertainment.'

Conversation died down when Emily was led in to the courtroom by Whertman and several deputies. She looked pale and drawn. Buck hoped to catch her eye but Emily only stared at the floor in front of her as she was led to her seat.

Every one was told to rise and a tall, elderly man draped in black, entered and made his way to the bench.

'Court is now in session,' the judge said and rapped the bench sharply with his gavel. He looked bored as he sank back into the heavily padded chair behind the bench.

'Before we proceed,' he wheezed, 'I want to remind all of you spectators who chew, about the spittoons at each end of the row. If I catch anyone spittin' on the floor of this court, I will fine him a dollar. The clerk may proceed.'

The clerk read the charges against Emily and then she was brought before the bench.

'How do you plead?' Judge Clarke asked.

Emily's reply was so soft that no one could hear her.

'Speak up, girl,' the judge ordered. 'Do you plead guilty or not guilty?'

'Not guilty,' Emily said. Her answer was just barely audible to the spectators.

'Where's her attorney?' Buck whispered to Lucero. 'Why doesn't she have counsel present?'

'There is no lawyer for her,' Lucero told him softly, 'she is not an 'Americano'!'

Buck was shocked. Even the lowest enlisted man in the army was always represented, if by no else than a junior officer. This was a travesty of justice. He stood up.

'May I address the court?' A murmur

ran though the crowd. The judge banged his gavel and called for quiet in the courtroom. Lucero tugged at Buck's arm, trying to get him to sit back down.

'Who are you?' Judge Clarke asked, when the crowd quieted.

'Captain Buck Buchanan, United States Army.'

The marshal went over to the judge and whispered something to him.

'Marshal Whertman says you're the fellow who brought this girl in after she and her father tried to shoot Clay Youngblood up in the mountains.' The judge looked sternly at Buck. 'And he tells me that you've killed at least one man here in Sante Fe and are walking around free only because there no witnesses to prove it was other than self-defense.'

'Miss Valdez was shot in cold-blood by J.W. Russell, Your Honor, and left for dead.'

'Did you see it?' Judge Clarke asked sharply.

'No, but I found her and found tracks that . . . '

'There are witnesses here in this courtroom,' the judge interrupted, not letting Buck finish, 'who did see what happened.' He looked smugly at Buck. 'I don't think you have anything to tell the court that will help one way or the other.'

'At least the court can appoint a lawyer to defend her!' Buck was trying to keep his anger under control.

'The court will decide if she needs counsel or not.' The judge turned to Whertman. 'Marshal, if this man interrupts again, you are to arrest him for contempt and take him to jail!' Then the judge beckoned for Whertman to come closer and he whispered something to the marshal who nodded his head yes.

'Now,' the judge said, looking around the courtroom, 'let the trial proceed without any more interruptions.'

Buck's worst fears were realized. Several of J.W.'s cronies testified that

Emily had walked into Webster's and gunned down a very innocent J.W. There was no defense, no cross-examination. Emily was called to the stand to tell her side. She spoke so low that almost no one could hear her. Judge Clarke didn't seem to mind and Buck was sure that the judge didn't care what she had to say.

In the end, Emily was found guilty and sentenced to be hanged at sunrise in three days. Buck was outraged and only Lucero's restraining arm prevented him from standing up and protesting such an obvious sham.

'You can't help her at all, if you are in jail, too!' Lucero whispered urgently.

Lucero stayed with Buck as a shaken Emily was led out and the courtroom cleared.

'I'm sorry, Señor Buck, but there was nothing you could do.' Lucero looked around to make sure they were alone. 'It has been rumored for some time that Judge Clarke is part of the group that wants the Valdez land. This was their chance to get her out of the way.'

'But why hasn't someone done something about this, exposed these men for what they are?'

'People who speak up have a way of disappearing,' Lucero said, 'and bad things sometimes happen to their families.'

'Well, we can't just stand by and let them hang her!'

'I agree, but do you have something in mind?'

'Yes, my old commander is now in Washington, D.C. I shall wire him to stop this hanging and to request a full investigation into the land dealings of all those involved.'

'Señor Buck,' Lucero said with some skepticism, 'I hope your friend is very high up because these people's influence goes a long way. What is his name?'

'Roosevelt,' Buck said. 'President Theodore Roosevelt.'

★ ★ ★

Buck found the telegraph office located in a small adobe building on a side street leading away from the plaza. Inside, at a desk behind a counter dividing the small room, a man sat reading a newspaper. On the desk was a telegraph key.

'I need to send a telegram,' Buck told him.

'Paper and pencil are in the box at the end of the counter,' the man said, not looking up from his newspaper. 'Write out your message.'

Buck did as directed. As he wrote he briefly outlined what had happened to him and Emily. He asked the President for a stay of Emily's execution and a full investigation into the murder of her father as well as a complete investigation into the land dealings of Russell and his associates.

'Here,' he told the operator.

The man folded his paper and came to the counter. He picked up Buck's message.

'This is a long one,' he snapped at

127

Buck, 'and it's going to cost a lot. Let's see where it's going.' His eyes widened and he looked up at Buck. 'The President of the United States? You want to send a telegram to the President of the United States?'

Buck just nodded yes and the man's face reddened.

'This is some kind of a joke!' he said, his voice getting loud. 'Well, mister, I'm not falling for it. Here!' He tossed Buck's message back across the counter. 'Now get out of my office!'

All of the day's frustrations, the trial, Emily's death sentence and now the rudeness of the telegraph operator, caused Buck to finally lose his temper.

He reached swiftly across the counter and grabbed the smaller man by his shirtfront and lifted him halfway across the counter.

'Your job is to send telegrams,' Buck said menacingly through his teeth, 'and I have a telegram for you to send. So just do your job.'

'Yes . . . yes, sir,' the operator

stammered. His face was no longer red but white with fright.

Buck let him go and the operator almost fell over the counter. When he had regained his balance, Buck handed him the message.

'Now, send it.'

The operator hurried to his key and in a few minutes Buck's message had gone out. Buck paid and then walked over to a bench near the door.

'I'll just wait here for the reply,' he said and sat down.

Several hours passed and the only activity was routine line tests. The operator tried to read his newspaper, but was too nervous to concentrate on it. He kept glancing over the tops of the pages at Buck.

Buck for his part, leaned back against the wall and waited. Finally, a long message came in. The operator copied it down, then handed it to Buck.

'It's from the White House,' he said in disbelief. 'Now who would have thought?'

Buck read the message, which was to Captain Buck Buchanan from the Secretary of War. The President was in a hospital, the message explained, in New York City. He had been injured, not seriously, in a carriage accident. However, it would probably be a week before he could respond to Buck's request. The Secretary was sure, however, that the President would take swift action once he learned of the plight of his former *aide-de-camp*. It was a start, Buck thought, as he crumpled the message and tossed it into a trash can. But he would have to buy Emily some time . . . but how?

Buck returned to his hotel and found his door unlocked. In the dim hallway, he could see light coming out from under his door. Someone was in his room. He drew his revolver, took a deep breath, then threw open the door and leaped in. In the middle of his bed sat Alice with nothing on but a sheet drawn close about her and a startled look on her face.

'Alice, what are you doing here?' He let the hammer down on the revolver and holstered it. Then he became angry with her. 'I almost shot you!'

'Come in and shut the door.' Alice told him, as she recovered from her fright. 'No use letting the whole hotel know you have a guest.' She let the sheet fall away and came to him. 'I've not seen anything of you because of that dreadful trial.'

Alice reached up to put her arms around him, but he tried to back away. She was a beautiful woman and at one time Buck had been a willing lover, but tonight, with Emily facing death, Buck felt no desire for Alice.

Alice pulled and tugged on him, trying to move him in the direction of the bed. It was at that moment that Buck saw the end of a rifle barrel come through the curtains over the window. He swept Alice up in his arms and kissed her long and hard, making sure she was between him and the window. His drawing his gun was hidden from the would-be assassin by her lovely body.

In one quick motion he threw Alice aside and fired into the curtains. There came a choking sound and then the heavy thud of someone falling to the ground. Alice went white. She looked at the smoking gun in Buck's hand and then fainted.

Buck heard shouts in the hallway and someone pounded on his door. He pulled a sheet up over Alice then went to the door. It was the desk clerk. Buck stepped into the hall and pulled the door shut behind him.

'Someone out on the patio tried to shoot me,' Buck explained, 'Come on!' He led the clerk and other guests who had come to investigate the shooting, through a door in the hallway that opened out on to the patio.

A man lay slumped under the window of Buck's room. Someone held up a lantern and the clerk examined the gunman.

'He's still alive,' the clerk announced.

'Someone run and get Doc. And somebody else go get the marshal.

'Do you know him?' the clerk asked Buck.

'No, do you?'

'Yes,' the clerk said, shaking his head in disbelief. 'This is Snyder, one of Whertman's men!'

Buck remembered the judge whispering something to Whertman at the trial. He wondered if it was about this. He went back to his room. He was not surprised to find Alice gone. Just as well, Buck thought. He quickly jammed his few belongings down into his saddle-bags and hurried out.

★   ★   ★

The walk to Colonel Russell's house seemed longer than usual. Neddy made the walk every evening after dinner, in order to help his boss and mentor review events of that day and plan for the next. And, Neddy had to admit, he enjoyed Russell's company. But tonight

133

he felt tired. Perhaps it was the Valdez girl's trial.

Neddy had watched Buck during the trial. His friend hadn't changed after all these years. Buck had been an idealistic cadet, believing in such silly things as justice, fair play and even the cadet's code of honor. But Neddy knew better. He had grown up in New York City.

Neddy's father had made a fortune in the publishing business. While Neddy was at West Point, that fortune had been stolen by his father's business partners. The courts would do nothing. His father had been unable to cope with his downfall and had disappeared. Neither Neddy nor any of the rest of the family ever saw him again.

No, Neddy thought, as he rang the colonel's doorbell, justice belongs only to the wealthy and the powerful. Justice belongs only to those who can afford to tip the scales in whatever direction they wished.

Russell's maid let Neddy in. The

Colonel was in his drawing-room. On the table in front of him was a half-full bottle of brandy and a shot glass. He didn't look up as Neddy came in.

'What happened in court?'

'The Valdez girl was found guilty and is to hang in three days.'

'Good,' the colonel said, and set his brandy snifter down. 'That's one of my son's killers taken care of.'

'I don't understand, sir.'

'Your friend, Captain Buchanan, is also to blame. If it weren't for him, J.W. would still be alive.'

'But, Colonel, he just happened along; it was an accident that he became involved.'

There was a knock at the door and then Marshal Whertman came in. He was clutching a piece of paper.

'Colonel, you got to see this. That son-of-a-bitch Buchanan wired the President.' Whertman showed the telegram Buck sent and the reply he got back.

'We have some time,' Russell said, as

he poured himself another shot of brandy. 'The telegram says something about a week, but the Valdez girl hangs in three days.'

6

The only light along the dark main street came from the jail. Buck quickly crossed the shadow-filled plaza and stopped in front of the jailhouse door. He adjusted the bundle under his arm and then went in. The bright yellow light from two kerosene lamps on the back wall temporarily blinded him and then his eyes adjusted.

A deputy marshal sat behind a desk in front of the back wall. As the man rubbed sleep from his eyes, Buck recognized him from the trial. His name was Miller.

'What d'ya want?' Miller's voice sounded harsh, like a man suddenly wakened and who really wanted to go back to sleep. Then Miller saw it was Buchanan and sat up straight. The marshal said certain people in town wanted Buchanan dead and everyone had been looking for him.

'I brought the girl some clothes,' Buck said, 'so she'll have something clean to wear tomorrow.'

'Leave 'em and we'll see that she gets them,' Miller said. He would wait until Buchanan turned around to walk out and then shoot the bastard.

But as Buck walked over to the desk, he noticed that the top right drawer was pulled open. From where he stood he could see the handle of a Colt Peacemaker. He bent over and put the bundle of clothes on a chair in front of the desk. Miller had to lean over the desk to see what he was doing. Buck reached into the bundle of clothes and found the handle of his service revolver. He straightened up suddenly, his gun at arm's length and aimed at Miller's head.

'Whaaat . . . you can't . . . '

'Don't make a sound,' Buck told him.

Miller hesitated and glanced down at the desk.

Buck cocked his revolver and the sound of the Smith & Wesson's action being worked was deafening in the still room. Buck waited. He had nothing against this man, although Emily said he had been present when J.W. was shot. In any event, Buck meant to kill him if he went for the gun in the drawer.

Somewhere in the room a clock ticked off the seconds. Outside, back behind the plaza, a dog barked. Beads of sweat began to form on Miller's forehead. Finally, he slowly raised his big hands over his head and stood up.

'Walk over to the corner and put your hands up on the wall, as high as you can reach!' Buck told him.

Miller backed over toward the corner of the room as Buck watched him over the sights of the revolver. When the deputy had backed into the corner, Buck told him to turn around and face the wall.

'Now, reach up higher, stand on your toes,' Buck instructed.

The deputy glanced over his shoulder and saw that Buck still had his gun extended and aiming at him. The deputy stood up on his tiptoes and reached as high as he could. Only then did Buck relax. While keeping his gun trained on the deputy, he moved around the desk, withdrew the Colt from the drawer and stuck it in his belt. A big ring of keys and a pair of handcuffs were in the drawer behind the gun and Buck took these out also.

'We're going to go in to the cells now, and you're going to go first,' Buck explained to the deputy. Buck walked over and pressed the barrel of his revolver to the back of Miller's head.

'Keep your hands up, walk very slowly and you'll live through this night!'

Sweat was now dripping off Miller's large nose. He walked to the door leading to the cells and opened it. Then together he and Buck went slowly through the door.

On the wall, in the hallway in front of

the cells, burned a small lamp that cast just enough pale yellow light to allow a guard to check on prisoners within the cells. Slowly, Miller led Buck down the dim hallway. The first cell was empty and its door was open.

'Inside!' Buck told him. 'Sit down with your back to the bars.' Miller did as he was told.

'Now put your arms behind you, through the bars.' Buck handcuffed his arms and then put a gag on him.

Buck moved quickly down the hallway, looking in each cell. Emily was in the last one, lying on a cot with her back to the cell door.

'Emily,' he called softly.

'Who . . . Buck?' She got up and came to the door where Buck was busily trying first one key and then another on the key ring, trying to open the lock.

'What are you doing?' she asked, her eyes wide with surprise.

'I'm getting you out of here,' Buck said. Suddenly the key he was trying, turned and the lock clicked open. He swung the door back and Emily rushed into his arms.

'If you do this, they'll arrest you too and you'll be ruined,' she cried.

'I'm not going to let them hang you!' he said, holding the frightened girl close to him. 'You've not had a fair trial and I believe your story.'

'Is that the only reason?' she asked softly, her dark eyes looking up at him.

'No,' he said huskily.

Buck stood there, holding her in his arms for several seconds before Emily pushed away from him.

'But where can we go? What can we do? It's hopeless!' Her eyes glistened with tears.

Buck took her arm and guided her down the hallway toward the office.

'I'll tell you outside,' he said, motioning to the handcuffed and gagged deputy in the first cell. 'He can still hear well enough.'

In the office, Buck threw the keys back into the desk drawer. He opened the front door and quickly glanced out. The street was still empty and no one was in the plaza. Buck guided Emily out the door and swiftly crossed the plaza to the entrance of a small alleyway. At the end of the alley, a dark visaged man sat on a horse. Three other horses also stood waiting. Two had saddles and the third carried a large pack.

'This is my friend, Charlie McBride,' Buck said, as he lifted Emily up on one of the saddle horses.

'*Buenos tardes, señorita,*' the man said in a low, soft voice.

'Charlie and I have a plan and I think we have a good chance.' Buck said in a low voice as he swung up on to the other horse. 'I've wired Colonel Roosevelt, President Roosevelt now, asking for your trial to be set aside and a full investigation. But he's in the hospital and can't help us for a few days. So, we're going to find someplace safe until then.'

'*El Presidente?*' she asked in amazement. 'You know the President?'

'Yes,' his smile flashed in the moonlight, 'and he owes me a favor or two. And T.R. always pays his debts.'

'Oooh,' she exclaimed softly, then a note of despair crept back into her voice. 'I wish I could be as sure as you.'

McBride touched his spurs to his horse and led the way at a quick walk. The night was clear and cold. The pungent, pleasing odor of piñon smoke hung in the air. Nothing stirred and everything was quiet except for the dull thuds of their horses' hoofs as they rode through the sleeping village. A dog barked at them and then quieted once they were past. They stopped at the edge of town and Buck checked cinches and their pack. A full moon hung high over the mountains to the east.

'It should be about one o'clock,' he told Emily as he checked the cinch on her saddle. 'I figure that we've about four maybe five hours' head start on the posse that's sure to follow, once they figure out which way we've gone.'

'Buck, I'm very cold,' Emily said in a

small voice. The chill seemed to cut through and settle in her wounded shoulder as a deep, dull pain.

Buck looked up and saw that all she had on was the thin dress that she had worn at the trial.

'I'm sorry,' he said, and quickly slipped off his own coat and handed it up to her. 'Here, put this on.'

He held her horse's head while she slipped his coat over her shoulders. It was much too large and she looked like a child dressing up in its parent's clothes. But she would be warmer.

'Better?' he asked.

'*Sí*,' came the reply, again in that funny small voice. She bent down and Buck felt her lips brush his cheek and then she straightened in the saddle.

They took the trail north towards Colorado for several miles then McBride turned due west. The land rose gently and by first light they were picking their way through rocky hills covered with sage brush and stunted juniper bushes. The sun came up a fiery red over the

Sangre de Cristo Mountains to the east. Emily thought how this very minute she would have been taking her last steps up to the gallows, but for the man riding so tall and proud in front of her. She realized how very much she had come to love this strange gringo, who was constantly saving her life. And to think that he was a personal friend of *El Presidente* . . . and that he loved her.

She pulled his jacket close about her shoulders and rode after him. He seemed so confident. She wished she could feel that way. Everything seemed so hopeless. And she couldn't help thinking that Buck had ruined his life, his future because of her.

★   ★   ★

A few hours after daylight, McBride reined his horse in at the edge of a deep rocky gorge about twenty miles west of Sante Fe. Buck and Emily looked down at the bottom. Some 600 feet below ran the Rio Grande River. On the far side of the river, rising like a giant pale fortress stood a great plateau. According to McBride, it was called the Pajarito Plateau that fanned out in a great arc from the dark blue Jemez Mountains rising to the west several miles away.

'This is White Rock Canyon,' Emily exclaimed, as she realized where they were. 'To cross, we have to go thirty-five miles north to Buckman or south thirty miles where Sante Fe Creek runs into the Rio Grande!'

'That's what most people think,' McBride told her. They were the first words she had heard him utter since leaving Sante Fe. He pointed north. 'There's a way down into the canyon less than a mile, up that way. It's an old Indian trail.'

Buck pulled out a map and was studying it. 'I think we're here,' he said, as he looked back and forth from the map to the surrounding terrain. 'Come and look,' he said to Emily.

'I'm sorry,' she stammered in embarrassment. 'I don't know maps.'

Buck saw a wave of scarlet cross her face. 'Can you read?' he asked. His voice was soft and he didn't want to embarrass her more.

'Oh yes!' She brightened. 'Before marrying my father, Mama was in a convent down in Chihuahua. There she learned to read and write, and to do numbers. She helped Papa keep his accounts. Mama taught me. I read and write Spanish, English and some Latin.' She held her head high. 'And I do numbers. I kept Papa's books after we lost Mamma and the others . . . '

A shadow of sorrow played moment-arily across her face. 'But where did you get your map?'

'From a fellow in the army . . . in Cuba.' Buck explained, as he carefully folded the map and put it away in his saddle-bag. 'His name is Brian McCain. At nights in the hospital, he used to talk about New Mexico and his ranch, hidden up a sunny canyon in the Jemez Moun-tains. The way he described it . . . a small clear stream full of trout in the bottom of the canyon, thickets of willow and alder, deer, bear and turkey . . . it made me want to come out here and see it. Maybe even get a ranch like that for myself. Anyway, he gave me this map of the territory. His ranch lies south of here, that way.' Buck pointed toward a tall, hazy, purple butte far to the south-west. 'At least I think that is where it is.'

'And just who is he?' Emily nodded toward McBride.

Both she and Buck studied McBride for several seconds. He was average in height with a powerful build that time was starting to soften. An open vest framed the makings of a noble paunch, which hung over his large, silver belt buckle. His dark-brown hair, under the black, flat-brimmed Stetson, was pulled back and tied with red strings into a bun. The heavy, double woven blanket that he had worn wrapped about him during the night was now rolled up and tied behind his saddle.

Emily was concerned that Buck was placing their fate in the hands of someone she didn't know. The land was full of people who talked big, but in the end were nothing but hot air. Emily's father had dealt with this kind often, some were gringos, some were Mexicans and few were Indians. They came in all sizes, shape and races.

'He's a half-breed. His father was one of the old-time mountain men and his mother a Navajo Indian. His father is supposed to have a big ranch that covers a lot of the Jemez. His name is Randell Fortune, ever heard of him?'

'I thought you said your friend's name is McBride?'

'Yes, but he took his mother's name and has taken up many of her people's ways.'

'Oh,' Emily was satisfied with Buck's explanation. 'I've heard of Fortune. My father bought some sheep from him.'

They rode north along the rim of the canyon. A pair of eagles soared high above them, riding the updrafts coming up out of the gorge. Then McBride stopped and pointed to a tall, black, lava rock jutting up from the lip of the gorge. When they got closer to it, Emily saw a mark scratched into it, the image of a hand print.

'That's it,' McBride said, 'that's the sign that marks the head of the trail leading down to the river.'

Buck and Emily looked down but could see nothing that looked like a trail. The rim of the gorge seemed to drop off in a sheer rock wall for twenty, maybe thirty feet where it met a steep slope of talus and jumbled lava rocks. But on the other side of the protruding rock, McBride showed them a small, indistinct path that led down through a large crack in the wall of the gorge.

'Wait here,' McBride said. He dismounted. 'I want to make sure the trail hasn't been covered by any landslide or something.' He handed Buck the reins to his horse and the lead rope to their pack-horse. Then disappeared down the trail. A few minutes later he reappeared.

'The trail's still clear. But we had better dismount and lead the animals,' he told them. 'The trail looks like it hasn't been used for many years, so be careful.'

McBride tied the pack-horse's lead rope to the tail of his horse and started down, leading both horses. Buck waited a few minutes for his friend to get ahead a ways and then started down with his big dun. Emily watched them disappear down into the crack of the wall. She took a deep breath, crossed herself and then started down with her own horse.

The trail was steep, narrow and frightening. The horses knocked stones loose, which plunged down the slopes, starting small avalanches. Then the trail reached the bottom of the rock wall and ran south along the top of the talus slope. Several times the pack bumped up against the sheer wall, causing the pack-horse to stumble on the narrow trail. Once it lost its footing and his hindquarters went over the edge of the trail. The horse scrambled frantically to get back up but the talus gave way beneath its feet. McBride's horse gave a mighty heave down the trail and pulled the pack-horse back up. Buck looked back at Emily, whose face was white with fright.

Finally, they turned a corner and the dim trail flattened out into a series of switchbacks going down the talus slopes. Buck looked up but could not see the rim of the gorge. Whoever made this trail had taken care to see that it was well hidden from view from above.

At last they reached the bottom of the gorge and the river. McBride stopped to rest the horses, letting them drink and nibble at the grass growing along the narrow sandy riverbank. Buck and Emily sat in the shade of a large, water-polished lava boulder and ate some of the food they had brought from Sante Fe.

Buck thought about how idyllic this spot might have been in different circumstances. The river here was a dark, brownish-green. The red and brown walls of the gorge rising behind them were laced with seams of black volcanic rock. He studied the other side of the river while they ate. The walls on the side were a light, cream color, from which the gorge got its name, White Rock Canyon. Directly across from them opened up the narrow mouth of a side canyon. A small stream issued forth, emptying itself in the greater river. Here, the Rio Grande was wide, shallow and muddy.

After they had finished eating, Buck led the way across the river. Emily's horse balked at the water and she had to kick it repeatedly in the ribs to make it cross. The effort caused her shoulder to burn deeply and she almost fainted. Buck was already on the other side, waiting for her.

When she caught up to him, she said through teeth clenched against the pain, 'If I had spurs on, this *caballo* would learn to fly across the water.'

Buck helped Emily off her horse and sat her down in the shade of a small cottonwood tree.

'Charlie and I are going ahead for a little while, maybe thirty minutes or so,' he told her. 'Just stay here and rest. If you need me just yell.'

With that, he and McBride left Emily and their pack horse. She lay back in the shade and shut her eyes. She felt warm. It seemed she had only closed her eyes for a second when she heard the sound of horses coming. She sat up and saw Buck coming out of the entrance to a small canyon. She got up and mounted her horse. As she did she glanced up at the rim and a cold chill swept through her. On the rim, silhouetted against the sky were two riders. Even as she watched, one turned his horse back away from the rim and disappeared. The other started down the dim trail toward the river.

7

At dawn Colonel Russell was just getting dressed so he could go enjoy the hanging when someone started pounding on his front door. He finished buttoning up his trousers and then went downstairs, muttering to himself about where were the servants when you needed them. Then he remembered that Sarah had given them the day off.

Russell opened the front door and found Neddy Vanders and Marshal Whertman.

'There's been a jailbreak,' Whertman said, 'Vanders' friend Buchanan busted the Valdez girl out and they took off!'

'Did you expect them to stay around and wait for you to arrest them?' Russell saw that his sarcasm was wasted on Whertman. The marshal expected the colonel to be livid with rage, but he was calm. Even Neddy was surprised at how calmly he was taking the news.

'You might as well come in and tell me everything,' Russell said, 'especially what you're doing about it . . . you are doing something, aren't you, Marshal?'

'Yes, sir,' Whertman said, as he and Vanders followed Russell into the study.

'Just what are you doing?' Russell motioned for Whertman and Vanders to be seated.

'I sent my people out in pairs to ride a big circle around Sante Fe in order to cut Buchanan's trail. When they do, and they're sure of the direction Buchanan took, one man is to keep on their trail and the other is to ride back to town where I'll be waiting with a posse.'

'Good,' Russell said. 'You've done well. Get Clay and his men for your posse. Now go back and wait. When someone comes in, come by for me.'

'You are unusually quiet, Neddy,' Russell said, after Whertman left.

'I'm just amazed at what Buck

. . . what Captain Buchanan has done. It's so unlike him. He was what we called a 'by-the-book' cadet and officer. He would have died before breaking any rules.'

'Yes,' the older man said, as memories of the War flooded his mind. 'We had officers like that too, the ones who were inflexible and, as a result, were broken, destroyed by the storm of battle. But Buchanan has proven to be more flexible and has mistakenly broken the law. It will take at least a week for any stay of execution to arrive here from Washington, maybe longer. And so we have a little time in which to maneuver.

'Send a wire to our friends in Washington,' Russell continued, 'and tell them to use whatever influence they have to stop any investigation, or at least hinder it until we can take care of your friend and the girl. Until we are told otherwise, she is still an escaped murderer and Buchanan is aiding and abetting her. No one can fault us should they be gunned down in a running fight with our posse. Buchanan has played right into our hands.'

* * *

Deputy Marshal Jake Miller was wet with sweat and in a foul mood by the time he reached the bottom of the gorge. Miller, who had something of a reputation as a horseman, had been forced to dismount and lead his big gray stallion down several narrower parts of the trail when the animal balked in fear.

'Should'a never bought ya,' Miller drawled, as he followed the trail left by Buchanan and the girl. There were two other horses with them. Probably pack-horses, Miller thought to himself.

The deputy was amazed that Buchanan had done nothing to hide the trail he and the girl had left. Miller thought that the least Buchanan should have done was stick to rocky ground so as to make trailing them a harder job.

'Stupid dude,' Miller muttered. He

was looking forward to getting his big hands on Buchanan and teaching him a lesson. No one pulled a gun on Jake Miller and got away with it. No, he would teach him a lesson that would stay with him the rest of his life, however long or short that was.

At the river's edge, Miller's horse stopped and lowered its head to drink. Miller savagely jabbed his spurs into the horse's flanks and jerked up on the reins.

'Come on, damn ya!' he yelled at the horse. 'You don't drink till I tell ya to!'

His shouting confused the big gray and it shied away from the gurgling water. It was only by much spurring and hitting the animal's flanks with the end of the reins that Miller got it across the river. As the horse hauled out on the other side, its flanks were badly gashed from Miller's big Mexican-rowled spurs. The horse stood there, its eyes rolling with fear of the man on its back.

'You're not worth the forty dollars I paid for ya, ya nag,' Miller said loudly, as he continued to berate the terrified horse. Clay Youngblood had brought the horse down to a corral in the foothills east of Sante Fe after he and his gang had returned from a trip south to El Paso.

'He's Mexican,' Youngblood had said. Miller was taken with the stallion. 'And everyone knows they raise the best horses in these parts.'

Miller didn't ask to see a bill of sale for the horse. He gave Youngblood forty dollars, a month's salary, and took the animal home. The big gray proved to be fast and have tremendous endurance. Unfortunately, the animal was high spirited and Miller's heavy-handed beat-'em and break-'em style of training wasn't working out.

'Should'a only paid five,' he concluded, as he followed the fugitives' trail along the river and through the narrow entrance to a high-walled side canyon. A small stream played through the bottom of it and the trail led into it but nothing came out, that Miller could

161

see. 'Little late,' Miller chuckled, 'to try and hide your trail. You can't go any way but up the canyon.'

Miller slowly followed the stream. The canyon floor was a maze of alder thickets mixed with clumps of willow and stands of cottonwood trees; all the leaves were in various shades of autumn browns, golds and yellows. Game trails led off from the stream into the brush. Miller noted fresh deer spoor, and turkey tracks were everywhere along the stream banks.

Just as he was rounding a large, thick clump of alders, Miller caught a glimpse of something glittering and whirling in the sun. And then it crashed into the side of his head. He was vaguely aware of falling from his horse and then his head hit the ground and he slid into blackness.

★ ★ ★

Marshal Whertman and his posse entered the canyon late that afternoon.

He wasn't surprised that they had been able to track the fugitives so easily. In his long years as a lawman, he found that most lawbreakers thought that by running hard, they could make good their escape. Few ever attempted any subterfuge. And Deputy Miller had also marked the trail for the posse. Whertman felt almost content.

'We'll have them before long,' he called out to the colonel who was riding beside Vanders nearby. 'I personally want to put the rope around Buchanan's neck.'

Youngblood, who was also riding nearby, smiled to himself. Buchanan wouldn't live long enough to see a rope.

'Don't get too cocky,' Neddy told Whertman. 'Buchanan is a a born tactician, one of the best in our class at the academy.'

'Aw, he ain't that much,' Whertman scoffed. As a young man, he had ridden with Quantrill's raiders. He considered himself something of a tactician himself.

'He got the girl out of your jail, didn't he?' Neddy countered. 'And he did so because you underestimated what Captain Buchanan would do.'

'Well, why didn't you warn us?' Whertman shot back. 'He's your friend and you are supposed to know him.'

'Gentlemen,' the colonel said, 'bickering will get us nowhere.' The colonel reined in to rest for a minute. 'Don't anyone underestimate Buchanan. He is strong, smart, and seemingly of great endurance. And he has killed four men who have tried to stop him.' No one said anything. 'Let us continue.'

★ ★ ★

Buck and Emily lay hidden in the brush at the entrance to a small grotto near the mouth of the side canyon. Their horses were well back in the thicket out of sight. McBride was with them to stop them from whinnying when the posse came by.

Buck felt Emily's nails dig into his

arm. 'They know we're here!' she said in a frightened whisper.

'No they don't,' Buck whispered back. 'Look, some of them are drinking from their canteens. They wouldn't do that if they thought we were close by. They'd be drawing weapons and maneuvering against us.'

'But how do you know they won't discover us?'

'Nothing is certain, but they won't discover that we've doubled back unless someone rides next to the canyon side.' Buck said softly, as he watched the last of the posse ride past and into the side canyon. 'But that's unlikely because they are so intent on following our trail and Miller's that they've not put out flank riders.'

When they couldn't hear the posse anymore, Buck rose and walked back to where McBride waited with their horses.

'They've passed us,' Buck told him. 'After I get what I need from the pack, take the horses and Emily back to the river and wait there for me.'

'How long should we wait?' Emily asked.

'I'll be about half an hour. You'll know when I'm on my way.'

★ ★ ★

The posse moved slowly up the canyon. As they rode, Neddy noticed that the canyon was becoming increasingly more twisted and narrower. They moved even slower. The canyon was perfect for an ambush. As they rounded a corner, someone let out a shout.

'It's a box canyon.'

Neddy pushed his way forward and saw that the canyon ended abruptly in a sheer cliff about 300 yards ahead.

'Look there, under that tree,' another rider shouted. 'Someone's tied to the trunk.'

'It's a trap!' one of Youngblood's riders called out.

Suddenly everyone dismounted and ran for cover in the rocks along the edge of the canyon wall. Neddy saw one of Whertman's men catch up the horses and lead them back around the bend, out of the line of fire. Strangely, no one was shooting at them.

'Ben! Jesse!' Whertman shouted. 'Cross over to the other side and work your way up toward the end. The rest of us will cover you!'

Neddy pulled a pair of field-glasses out of his coat pocket and examined the end of the canyon.

'It's Miller,' he told them. 'He's tied to a tree and gagged as well.' Neddy studied the rest of the canyon end. 'There doesn't seem to be anybody else there. At least there is no place to hide any horses.'

Neddy passed his field-glasses to the colonel who began to scan the area where Miller was tied. One of the men Whertman sent to the other side came running back out of breath.

'Four or five horses went back down the canyon,' he said between gulps of air. 'They were down in a gully which can't be seen from this side of the canyon because of all the saltbrush.'

The colonel got up, dusted himself off, and began walking by himself up the canyon toward Miller. Several men got up and followed.

'Gawd-almighty am I glad to see you boys,' Miller cried, when they removed the gag. 'Anybody got any water?'

Someone handed him a canteen and he drank deeply.

'Where's Buchanan and the girl?' Whertman demanded, and went on before Miller could say anything, 'and why in the hell can't you do anything right?'

'Let him finish his water, Marshal,' the colonel said. Everyone waited while Miller drank until he had drained the last drops from the canteen.

'Now, Deputy,' the colonel said, 'tell us what happened.'

'Well, Ben and me cut Buchanan's sign about two miles from the gorge's rim. I sent Ben back to get y'all.'

'We know that part,' Whertman said, 'get to where you met up with them.'

'Please, Marshal, let him tell it his own way.' The colonel listened patiently while Miller talked. Whertman and the others fidgeted around, only half listening as Miller told of how easy it had been to trail Buchanan, of following him down to the river and into the side canyon.

'I was just around the bend coming through that narrow place when Buchanan hit me over the head,' Miller explained. 'When I came to, I was tied to this tree.'

'Had'a been me I would have killed you!' Whertman said. 'Only an idiot lets himself be ambushed.'

'Buchanan said he had a message for Mr Vanders,' Miller said, ignoring the marshal.

This surprised Neddy. 'What message?'

'Buchanan said to go home. He said he didn't want to have to take to the field against you.' Miller looked up at Neddy. 'Do you know what he was talking about?'

'It means he doesn't want to fight us.'

'Well,' Miller shook his head, 'for somebody not wanting to fight he sure has a lot of guns an' stuff . . . he's even got a couple of boxes of dynamite on his pack.'

'Dynamite?' the colonel said. 'We've made a big mistake, gentlemen! Get on your horses and ride out of this canyon as fast as you can!'

Everyone rushed for his horse. Amidst the confused scramble, Neddy found his black gelding and started back down the canyon. The colonel and Marshal Whertman were just ahead of him. Neddy thought they were four or five miles from the canyon's mouth and it would probably take fifteen or twenty minutes to get out. But he doubted they could get there in time. Buck could blow the wall down on them anywhere in the canyon before they got to the narrow entrance.

And then he knew what Buck was thinking: he didn't plan on killing them here in the canyon, he was simply going to blow up the entrance and trap them inside. Neddy touched his spurs to his gelding urging the horse to go faster.

★   ★   ★

McBride and Emily sat in the shade of a tall willow tree growing next to the river. Their horses were tied up short, ready to go, under a nearby cottonwood. This was the first time Emily had a chance to study the Indian. He sat with his back against the tree, eyes closed as if sleeping, but Emily could tell he was awake and listening intently to the sounds around them. Emily listened too, but all she heard was the river gurgling as it rushed over and around the many rocks that had fallen from the side of the gorge and tumbled down into the river bottom.

'*Señor*,' she said, breaking the quiet, 'how is it you know Señor Buchanan?'

'Ai,' McBride said, opening his eyes and looking at her. 'That is a long story, some parts sad and some parts happy.'

He pulled a short, stubby little pipe out of a small pouch tied to his belt, filled it with tobacco and lit it.

'Captain Buchanan was one of our leaders in Cuba,' McBride said between puffs. 'He is a special man, your captain.'

Emily felt her cheeks redden. Were her feelings for Buck so apparent to everyone?'

'If he were an Indian, he would be a great warrior,' McBride said. 'But then the whites would kill him because he would be too dangerous to them.'

Emily said nothing; she just listened as McBride told her about Cuba, the Roughriders and Buck Buchanan.

'The captain cares for people and is always serving others as best he can. Time and again he risked his life to go to the aid of wounded soldiers. He is a very brave man and also as cunning as an old coyote.'

Emily remembered all that he had

done for her, the risks he had taken and was taking for her.

Suddenly she was jolted out of her reverie by a tremendous explosion in the direction of the entrance to the side canyon. It was followed by two more blasts in quick succession and then Buck was there, telling her to mount up and follow.

★　★　★

Over the pounding of the horses' hoofs, Neddy and the rest of the posse also heard the explosions. When they rounded the last turn leading to the entrance, the canyon was filled with dust. And there, where the canyon narrowed the most, was a massive wall of jumbled rock which Buck had blasted down from overhanging canyon walls.

'What'll we do now?' someone hollered. 'Our horses can't climb over that!'

'We are going to leave our horses and

climb out of here,' the colonel said. 'And we must take our saddles and everything else we can carry.'

It took the posse over three hours of hard work to get everything out of the side canyon and down to the river.

'Now, we're going to wait here while Marshal Whertman walks back to town for horses.' Russell glared at Whertman. 'Isn't that right, Marshal?'

'Yes, Colonel.' Whertman knew it was no use arguing. He looked around at the rest of the posse. 'Anybody else want to come with me?'

Neddy was surprised that several others volunteered to go along. Maybe it was better than sitting there by the river, and waiting.

'How long do you think it will take them to get to town and back?' Russell asked Neddy.

'About nine, maybe ten hours,' Neddy said. He pulled out his watch and studied it. 'It's now twenty past three so I wouldn't expect them back until midnight or after.'

'That's my estimate, too.'

'Buck apparently has a guide now, someone who knows this country very well,' Neddy said.

'We can play that game, too. When we get our horses we'll go back to Sante Fe and then start looking for a renegade Indian who will know where Buchanan's guide is taking them.'

'You know that Buchanan has succeeded in neutralizing us?' Neddy asked, but the colonel said nothing. 'Buchanan has gained time to escape effective pursuit. And when we get back to town,' Neddy went on, 'we had better start preparing for the investigation Buchanan requested.'

'Yes, yes,' the colonel finally said, waving his hand at Neddy as if to dismiss all that he had said. 'The right people in Washington have been contacted. We must take our problems as they come. Right now we must concentrate on getting Buchanan and the girl. They must not live to testify against us. Do you understand how important that is?'

Neddy nodded his head.

'Good. When we get back, I want you to put the word out that I'll pay two thousand to the man who kills Buchanan and another thousand for the girl!'

8

Buck found Emily and McBride waiting in the shade of a tall cottonwood, about two miles downriver from the side canyon. 'They won't trouble us any more today,' Buck told them.

'What did you do to them?' Emily asked. Buck told her about dynamiting the entrance to the canyon and she shook her head in wonder.

'Where are you taking us?' Buck asked McBride.

'It's a long four-day ride from here, because we have to go around the Jemez,' he said, pointing to the mountains west of them. They followed the river downstream for several miles. From there, McBride headed them west, up another side canyon that led out to the base of the large plateau they had seen earlier.

'The Pajarito Plateau,' McBride explained,

during a halt to rest the horses, 'runs along the south-east side of the Jemez range. We'll follow the edge of the plateau around to the south side of the mountains, then head west along the foothills until we hit canyon country.'

But progress was slow. The country was rough and broken by a great many washes and deep arroyos with steep banks. Much time was lost finding places across them. Gnarled and stunted junipers and piñon pine dotted the hillsides. The open areas between the trees were covered with sparse stands of thin grasses and patches of cholla. Buck made the mistake of riding too near a cholla and felt a sharp, burning pain as his lower leg brushed against the branching, stick-like bush. He had to dismount and pull the round spine-covered pads from his leg. The white-hot pain made him break out in a cold sweat. Afterwards, he took more time in picking his way through the cholla.

As evening approached, the light tan

hills took on the crimson hues of the brilliant sunset. To their north, the white bluffs of the plateau were washed with a delicate pink, as the sky went from blood red, to a more subtle purple, streaked with varying shades of vivid orange. Buck was deeply impressed by this display of stark beauty.

All too soon, the kaleidoscope of sunset faded out into the black of night. Still, McBride led them on. Emily swayed in her saddle, but clung tightly to her saddle horn to avoid falling off. Buck could feel himself becoming more exhausted with each passing hour. He guessed that it was close to midnight when McBride led them into a wash at the foot of a small cliff.

'We'll camp here,' McBride said. 'It's out of the wind and no one will see our fire.'

Buck dismounted and went to help Emily down. She was so stiff from the long ride that she could barely walk. While Buck unloaded the pack horses, McBride started a small fire in an old stone fire ring that looked like it had seen much use at one time. 'Have you camped here before?' Buck asked.

'No,' McBride said. He laid more dry sticks on the small fire. 'It's an old camp my mother's people used on their way to raid the Spaniards south of here, along the river. My uncle used to tell us stories about the raids and mentioned this place.'

And that is why, Buck thought, the army had such a hard time catching Indian raiding parties. Someone had been there before and told everyone else. Each Indian carried a map, a detailed word map of their part of the world. Each generation refined that map and then passed it on to the next generation. Waterholes, hunting grounds, ambush sites, sanctuaries deep in the mountains, the whole terrain and how to use it, was there in those stories. Most Indians couldn't read or write, but they remembered everything they saw and heard. McBride's people, the Navajo, were a good example.

Supper was just tortillas and some jerky McBride had packed. Emily ate very little. Buck spread a bedroll for her and she was soon asleep. He unrolled his own bedroll and the last thing he remembered was seeing McBride tending his little fire.

Buck felt someone shaking his shoulder. It was McBride. There was a golden glow of light in the east. It would be dawn soon. Buck got up and found that coffee had been made. While McBride went for the hobbled horses, Buck made breakfast, nothing fancy, just pancakes and biscuits. He and McBride did most of the eating. Emily refused anything but water and hardly spoke to him. She looked exhausted.

'How's your shoulder?' he asked her.

'OK,' she mumbled.

What they didn't eat, Buck put in a cloth sack and stashed in his saddlebags. It would have to do them for lunch. All day they rode slowly but steadily west. Little by little, the land changed from broken foothills and arroyos to more rolling hill country. The juniper and piñon pines were taller now. In the bottoms of the washes, and on cooler north-facing slopes, there were small stands of ponderosa pine. The tall peaks of the Jemez range were now directly to their north.

The riding was easier than the day before. There were fewer washes and arroyos to cross, which meant they could cover more ground. Shortly after sunset, they crested a hill and could see a small cluster of lights twinkling in the foothills at the base of the mountains.

'That's the village of Cuba,' McBride told them. 'We'll put some distance between it and us before we set up camp.'

Again, it was nearly midnight when he finally stopped along a small stream. The mountains were far to the north-east and they had entered a country of canyons and plateaus. Emily lay down on the bedroll Buck spread for her and was asleep before he could get food prepared.

'Let her sleep,' McBride told Buck. 'She's tired from all this.'

'I'm worried about her,' Buck told his friend. 'She didn't eat much today and seems to be getting weaker.'

'We'll get to this place I have in mind, tomorrow afternoon,' McBride said. 'Then she'll have all the time she needs to rest.'

'Do any other Navajos know about this place?'

McBride nodded his head yes.

'Then how do you know that one of them might not stumble across us and then tell Russell or Youngblood where we are?'

'Ghosts,' McBride said, and smiled at Buck's puzzled look. He took his small stone pipe out of his saddle-bag, and filled it.

'The place where I'm taking you is full of ruins of an ancient people,' he said. He took an ember from the fire and put it in the bowl of his pipe and sucked on it until it was lit. 'Navajos won't go there because they think that the spirits, the Chinle, of these people still live in the ruins. So no one should even know you're there.

'And,' McBride added, 'the few whites that run cattle or sheep there, have moved their stock out for the winter. You should be safe until spring.'

★   ★   ★

By noon the next day, McBride led them down into a maze of canyons. Many had small streams, bordered by cottonwood and willows, flowing along their bottoms. The red and yellow canyon walls of sandstone were steep and only now and then would Buck see a place where a man might climb out. He saw no way to get a horse in or out.

Just before dark, they came to a small stone cabin built into the base of a south-facing wall of a long, narrow canyon they had followed for the last two hours. McBride got down and went inside. Buck could hear him moving things around. Buck got down and went over to Emily to help her down.

'Well, this is it,' McBride said, coming back outside. 'This will be home for a while. Used to belong to a crazy old white man who was convinced the ancients had stored tons of gold in these canyons. He came in here every summer to look for it, but I don't think he's been here for several years. Must have died or just gave it up.'

With Buck's help, Emily dismounted. Her shoulder hurt. It wasn't a white-hot pain, like when she got shot. Instead, it was a dull ache that seemed to just wear her out. She was tired of riding, tired of worrying about being caught, even tired of being too exhausted to be of any help to herself. Everything was gone. Her family, her hopes, her dreams, everything. What, she wondered, through the fog of the pain and exhaustion which clouded her mind, was the use of going on? She felt her knees buckle under her and everything went black.

Buck caught her as she fell and

carried her inside the stone house. There, he laid her on some saddle blankets McBride had spread on a crude wooden bed.

'We've got to get her help,' Buck told McBride. 'Are there any towns where we can get a doctor?'

'No, but there's an old singer, what you whites call a medicine man, who has his hogan about a half a day's ride from here.'

'Could he really help her?' Buck was skeptical. 'I mean, could he give her medicine that would help her heal?'

'My friend,' McBride said, 'our people have used healers longer than anybody knows. They have learned much about sickness and healing that has been passed down for generations. I think he can help her.'

'I'm sorry.' Buck was embarrassed by having to be lectured. 'I didn't mean to presume that your doctors didn't know anything. Please try and find him.'

'If I leave now,' McBride said, 'I

might be able to have him back by noon tomorrow.'

For several minutes, Buck could hear McBride's horse going down the canyon, then all was still. He rummaged through his pack and found a candle. By its feeble light, he gathered enough brushwood for a fire. Once the fire was going inside, Buck brought in his pack and their saddles and stored everything neatly in a corner. Then he busied himself with cleaning out the cabin.

As he worked in the pale reddish light from the fire in the small stone fireplace, he found himself glancing over at Emily. She lay just as he had left her. He made a small pot of coffee then went over and checked on her. She felt hot to his touch and he felt fear. He had seen more than one wounded soldier come down with such a fever and then die.

He took his cup of coffee and went to sit on the floor next to her bunk, his back against the wall. Buck had never been very religious, but now he found himself sort of praying, asking God to help this girl recover, to let her live and be happy. Sometime near dawn he must have fallen asleep.

The sound of hoofbeats awakened him. He pulled his rifle from its scabbard and then peeked out the door. Two men were coming up the canyon. One was McBride. As they came closer, Buck was able to make out the other rider. He appeared to be a wizened old man.

'This is Hosteen Joe Begay,' McBride said in way of an introduction when they got to the cabin. Through McBride Buck told the old man what had happened to Emily and about her fever. Begay grunted then went into the cabin. McBride grabbed Buck by the arm and indicated for him to wait outside. They led the horses to an old corral and unsaddled them.

The old man came to the door and said something in Navajo to McBride. Buck's friend fetched Begay's saddlebags and took them into the cabin. In a few minutes he came back out.

'We need to build a small fire out here and heat some water,' McBride said. 'He's going to fix up a drink of tea, to kill the fever.'

They gathered wood and built a small, hot fire. McBride boiled water in an old coffeepot and took it into the cabin. His face was solemn when he came out.

'Joe says she's badly off, that her shoulder hasn't healed and she's worn out.'

'Can he help her?' Buck asked.

'He'll do what he can, but it may take a while.'

All day Buck and McBride waited in the shade of one of the canyon walls. Just before dark, McBride went into the cabin and brought out Buck's bedroll.

'Thanks,' Buck told him, 'but I don't think I'll be able to sleep tonight anyway.'

Together they waited outside in the dark. Buck thought the night would never end. They could hear the old man droning on and on, hour after hour, as he sang chant after chant. At last, dawn came and, as the morning light filled the canyon, Begay's chanting stopped. The old man came to the cabin door and motioned for them to come in. Emily was asleep. Her forehead was cool to Buck's touch. The fever was gone. Begay said something to him, but Buck couldn't understand and looked at McBride for a translation.

'He says the corruption in Emily's shoulder is gone, that the medicine did that. But he can't do anything for her spirit, which is out of balance with nature. Only you can help her spirit to mend so that it will be at peace and she can again live in harmony.'

Begay said something else, then held up two cloth packets.

'These are for Emily,' McBride translated. 'The one wrapped in the calico is for her shoulder. Make a compress from the leaves in it and put it on fresh each day.' Begay said something else. 'The other bag is for a tea, a couple of times a day.'

Buck followed McBride and the old man outside.

'Ask him what I owe him,' Buck said.

McBride did as he was asked. The old man said nothing, just caught up his horse and saddled it. Then he smiled at Buck, said something and laughed as he started his horse away at a fast walk.

'What did he say?' Buck wanted to know.

'He wants nothing for himself. But he said the girl can give his wife ten head of sheep when she's better.'

McBride saddled his own horse and led it out of the corral. He missed his wife and told Buck he needed to get back to his family.

'Not much I can do here,' he said. 'Time to go home. In a week or so, I'll ride over to Sante Fe and see what's going on.'

'When should I expect you back?'

'You'll be OK here for a while. There's deer up near the tops of the canyons, and maybe a few head of stray sheep down in the bottoms, that is if the coyotes or mountain lions haven't eaten them. You have plenty of flour, coffee and beans with you, so, I don't need to come back for five or six weeks.'

Buck watched his friend ride down the canyon until McBride disappeared around the corner at the far end. The sounds of his horse died away and an immense stillness seemed to fill the canyon.

*   *   *

Emily slept all day. Buck groomed the horses, fixed broken boards on the corral fence and had no trouble keeping himself busy. Tomorrow he would have to put up a makeshift fence across the lower end of the canyon so that the horses could be turned out to graze. Every half-hour he looked in on Emily to make sure she was all right. Toward dusk, she stirred and sat up.

'Hi,' Buck told her. He felt a wave of relief sweep over him. She was going to be all right! 'Are you hungry? I can get you something to eat.' Buck had a pot of stew keeping warm by the fireplace. Without waiting for her to answer, he fixed her a plate and set a couple of yesterday's biscuits on the edge.

Emily took a few bites of the stew, then set the plate down beside her. She didn't say anything, and just sat, staring at the floor. He felt his heart sink but tried not to make a show of it. He didn't want to push her and hoped that, with time, she could get herself together. They could always talk later.

Three days went by and Emily still sat on the bed, staring off into space. She didn't talk and only nodded her head yes or shook her head no when Buck asked her a question. The only time she got up was to go outside to relieve herself. By now, Buck was really starting to worry. He remembered what Joe Begay told him, that only he, Buck, could heal her mind and her spirit. The problem was, he had no idea of how to do it.

Desperation set in. Nothing he said or did seemed to help. By the fourth day, she was pale and drawn. Emily hadn't had much more that a few sips of water and even less to eat. Buck almost had to force her to drink Begay's tea.

Half in frustration and half in fear, he grabbed his rifle and stomped out of the cabin. He couldn't stand to see her wasting away. He felt so helpless. He remembered Major Benton telling stories of his time at the San Carlos Apache Indian Reservation. One of his best scouts learned that the Rurales in Mexico had killed the scout's brother, who was all the family he had left after so many years of warfare. The scout, who was called Jose, sat down in front of his wickiup and withdrew from the world. He didn't eat or drink but just sat staring, like Emily, at the ground. In six days he was in such bad condition that he was taken to the infirmary. Three days later he died. The other scouts told Major Benton that Jose died of despair, that with the loss of his brother, there was nothing for him to hope for.

Was that, Buck wondered, what was wrong with Emily? Maybe that was what Begay had meant about healing her spirit. He had to help Emily find hope, to give her something live for.

Buck headed up the canyon in search of game. As he walked, he willed himself to concentrate on hunting and to forget his worries. In this way, he hoped an answer might come to him. It had happened before. He watched closely for signs of deer and carefully studied the canyon floor and walls. He noticed that the canyon was made of different layers of sandstone. Some were dark red, while others were a soft yellow or almost white.

Here and there, Buck saw high up on the cliff faces what looked like sections of stone walls, laid up to seal off small caves. Then he rounded a corner and there was a group of three or four stone buildings snuggled up against the base of one of the canyon walls. McBride had said that an ancient race had lived in these canyons, a long time ago. But the old ones were gone and their cities were in ruins by the time the Navajo came to this part of the country. From the ruins, Buck continued up the canyon. He began to see the heart-shaped tracks of deer. About a mile further on, the canyon widened slightly, and a small grove of cottonwoods filled most of the canyon floor. A few golden leaves still hung from bare, gray branches. A large nest of twigs had been built high up in the fork of one tree. Buck guessed it had belonged to a raven or hawk.

As he neared the grove, he saw light reflecting off flowing water under the trees. Walking slowly and softly, Buck worked his way into the small grove. Hoofprints were everywhere. A few of the prints were different in a puzzling way from the other deer tracks. They were about the same size as those of the smaller deer, but narrower. They looked familiar, but he couldn't place them.

The stream was nothing more than a small trickle of water. He followed it through the grove and soon left the cover of the trees. The small trickle came from a spring flowing out of rocks near one side of the canyon. From that point, the canyon floor was just a dry wash of sand and rock.

Buck suddenly noticed movement, about a hundred yards up the canyon. A surge of excitement swept over him and he readied his rifle. Something grayish-tan was skulking around in a large circle. It was a coyote. Then Buck saw the creamy-white animal the coyote was circling. It was a sheep. The strange tracks in the grove were sheep tracks, and Buck laughed at himself for not recognizing them. The sheep was probably a stray, accidentally left behind by white ranchers or Navajo herders who grazed their flocks down near the lower end of the canyon in the summer.

As Buck watched, the coyote circled

its intended prey. But the sheep constantly turned to face its attacker. Then the coyote advanced toward the sheep, which stamped its foot and charged, head lowered, at the coyote. The coyote danced out of the way of the charge and darted into the center of the circle and nipped at something. Buck couldn't tell what. One quick nip was all the coyote had time for, because the sheep wheeled and drove the coyote back out from the center.

Both animals were so intent that neither heard Buck coming. At about thirty yards, he saw the object of the coyote's attack. A small lamb lay huddled behind its mother. Buck knew that the ewe would not be able to keep the coyote away from its baby much longer. In fact, Buck was surprised at the fight the ewe was showing. He was sure that the coyote was just as surprised and only that was what was saving the ewe and her lamb.

He raised his rifle and aimed at the coyote. He had nothing against the animal. Like everyone else, it was just trying to make a living. The thought made Buck smile. He lowered his gun.

'Hey!' he shouted. 'Hey you!'

At the sound of his voice, both animals skidded to a halt and stared at him.

'Get out of here!' he hollered, and shook his fist at the coyote.

The coyote laid its ears back and took off, running up the canyon. Buck laughed as he watched it quickly disappear around a bend.

But the sheep hadn't moved. It stood panting from exertion and fright. Its lamb lay frozen in fear, hugging the ground. Buck walked over to them.

'It's going to be all right, momma,' he said softly to the ewe.

She backed away nervously and ran off a few yards. Then she turned and watched him anxiously as he knelt and examined her baby.

'Just a few nips, little one,' he said to the lamb. He ran his hands over it, calming it. 'You'll be OK in a day or two. But we can't leave you out here as coyote bait.'

Buck slung his rifle from his shoulder and picked the lamb up. He would put them in the old corral at the cabin. They would be safe there.

'Come on, momma,' he told the worried ewe. 'Let's find you a home.'

Carrying the lamb, he started walking away, back down the canyon. The ewe stood and watched him go. She bleated to her lamb and then started following several yards behind.

★   ★   ★

It was dusk by the time Buck got the animals to the cabin and into the corral. He got some salve from his pack and started doctoring the lamb's injuries. Still anxious about her baby, the ewe bleated noisily. Buck was bent over the lamb when he heard someone come up behind him. It was Emily.

'I found them up the canyon,' he told her, 'and brought them home so they would be safe from the coyotes.'

Emily gave no sign that she even heard him. She simply took the lamb from him and, hugging it tight, slowly sank to the ground. She buried her face in the lamb's fleece, her shoulders shaking as she began crying.

Buck knelt down and put his arms around her. He found hope in the fact that she was up, not just sitting and staring at the walls of the cabin. Something had snapped her out of her depression. Who would have guessed that sheep would do that? Buck suspected that the sheep must have stirred up memories of her father's flocks, memories of him and all that she had lost, bursting the dams her mind had built to shut out her grief. Now that grief was washing over her like a great wave as she sat sobbing.

With the sun gone, the canyon was rapidly becoming cold.

'Let's go inside, Emily.'

If she heard, she gave no indication. As gently as he could, Buck took the lamb from Emily and returned it to its mother.

'Here, momma.' The ewe began to nuzzle the lamb, which began to nurse greedily. 'Your baby's all right now.'

He lifted Emily and carried her inside the cabin and sat her down on some saddle blankets then sat next to her. Far into the night he held her as she cried out her grief.

Shortly after midnight Emily stopped crying and went to sleep. Buck picked her up and carried her over to the bed. The little cabin was cold. Buck lit several candles and got a small fire going in the fire-place. Seeing that the wood box was almost empty, he went out for more wood. When he came back he saw that his bedroll had been moved. Emily was lying under her covers, watching him. Spread out next to her was his bedroll.

★ ★ ★

Snows came but soon melted in the sunny, sheltered canyons. Emily mended quickly and was a delight to Buck. Together they hiked the maze of canyons, exploring old ruins and gathering up what stray sheep they found. Soon their little flock had grown to a dozen ewes and lambs. Emily began taking them out daily to graze with the horses in the canyon. She also took Buck's little carbine to use on any coyotes trying to get dinner from her little flock.

The canyon abounded in small game. Buck set out snares and he and Emily feasted on roasted rabbit and quail. One day he brought home a turkey. While he plucked it, Emily dug a pit and built a fire in it. She also built another fire next to the pit. Much to Buck's horror, she covered the fresh turkey with an inch-thick layer of mud. When the fires had burned down, Emily placed the mud-covered turkey down on to the coals in the pit, then filled the pit with hot coals from the second fire. Then she covered everything with a layer of dirt.

'Tomorrow we will eat the best meal ever,' Emily told a doubting Buck.

The next day Emily dug up the cooked turkey. Buck was amazed as the rock-hard layer of mud peeled off, leaving a juicy cooked bird. Emily was right; it was the best turkey he ever ate.

Not long after, Buck shot a young fat buck. Emily sliced the venison into thin strips and hung them to dry on bushes near the cabin. The jerky she made would be their reserve food supply, something to fall back on if game became scarce and McBride was late in coming for them.

One afternoon, in early spring, Buck sat with his back against the cabin wall. Warmed by the sun, he felt content and at peace. Emily was up the canyon with her small flock. The canyon was quiet except for the gentle whispering of the wind across the canyon floor. Through his sleepy haze he became aware of a low rumbling sound, so faint that he could barely hear it. He lay down on the ground and pressed his ear against the hard, sun-baked earth and listened. Horses! And coming quickly. He ran into the cabin for his rifle and then hurried down the canyon to wait for the coming riders.

9

A quarter of a mile from the cabin, where the canyon floor was thick with big sage, he left the trail. About fifteen yards away from it, he lay down and blended into the shade of an old gnarled sagebrush that seemed too small to hide a man. Then he waited.

Five long minutes dragged by before two riders came around the bend at the far end, their horses at a fast walk. They were too far away for Buck to identify, but from the way they sat their horses, he was sure they were Navajos and they were in a hurry. As they came closer, he could see that one was a big man wearing a flat-brimmed black hat and riding a paint horse. It was McBride. The second rider was old man Begay. Buck let them ride past and then stood up and called to them.

'Hold on!'

Both riders brought their horses around sharply. And both men had guns out, pointing at Buck.

When he saw who it was, McBride grinned and holstered his gun. Old Man Begay said something to McBride and laughed.

'He says you'd make a good Indian,' McBride stepped his horse close to Buck. 'But he also says you're lucky he didn't come around shooting.'

As they walked their horses beside Buck up the trail to the cabin, McBride's tone became more serious.

'Where's the girl,' he asked. 'I don't see her about.'

'She's up the canyon with some sheep we found.' Buck could see that his friend looked worried. 'Why?'

'We've been betrayed!'

'What do you mean?' Buck stopped and asked. 'Betrayed by whom?'

'A relative of mine, a cousin, learned of Joe's visit here to doctor Emily. Now this cousin, on the promise of a lot of money, is leading Youngblood and his gang into the canyons. Russell, Vanders and the marshal are with them.'

'We must gather your things,' McBride said, 'and go, quickly. These men are not far behind us!'

While Buck got his pack together, McBride rode out for Emily. She was in tears when they returned.

'My sheep!' she cried. 'What's going to become of them? The coyotes will eat them!'

'I'm sorry,' Buck said. He held her close. 'There's nothing else we can do.'

Emily was furious. She went into the cabin for her things and the men could hear her throwing things around and muttering to herself. She wasn't any calmer when she finally emerged, a bundle under her arm.

'I hope I see Russell!' Emily told them. She held up Buck's carbine. 'He's the real coyote and I will shoot him!'

'You may get your chance very soon if we don't hurry,' McBride told her. 'We were only an hour or two ahead of

Russell and his men when we got to the canyons. And we have to back-track down to the main canyon to get to the other trail out.'

Begay brought in their horses and Buck loaded his pack-horse while McBride and Emily saddled the other two. Soon they were on their way at a fast walk down the canyon. They hugged the side, well away from the trail that ran out in the center of the canyon floor. Emily and Begay led the pack-horse while Buck and McBride followed, dragging brush tied to ropes behind them to wipe out their tracks.

'This won't fool anybody who rides down this side,' Buck told Emily, 'but it will stop our tracks from being so noticeable from the main trail. So, it might buy us a few minutes.'

It took them an hour to reach the main canyon. Begay turned north and the main canyon soon became a twisted maze. So many side canyons opened into the main one that Buck could no longer tell which was truly the main canyon.

As they rode, McBride brought Buck up to date on what had been happening in Sante Fe.

'Roosevelt must have gotten around to your telegram,' McBride told him. 'Sante Fe's like a hill of angry ants, crawling with federal marshals, special agents and federal investigators. The girl's trial,' McBride nodded at Emily, 'was thrown out and charges dropped.'

'Thank God for that,' Buck said. 'But what about Russell, Clarke, and the rest?'

'Judge Clarke, Russell, Vanders, Brock, Whertman, and most of the men who work for them, have been charged with conspiracy and a lot of other stuff. Enough to put them away for lots of years. Unfortunately, they were released on bail, until their trial.' McBride laughed. 'They were told not to leave town. A lot of good that did, because they all took off like rabbits running from a grass fire.'

'My friend,' McBride told Buck, 'everyone in Sante Fe knows that

Russell's sworn to kill you and the girl, for causing his ruin and to avenge his son's death. And now, my coyote cousin, Black Hand, is going to see that Russell gets a good shot at having his vengeance.'

They rode in silence for a while, then Buck asked, 'Where's Joe taking us?'

'Further into the canyons, towards the mountains in the north-west,' McBride explained. 'The old ones built a large village at the end of the canyon. I don't know where it is, but Joe first discovered it during the great round-up years ago, when he was a young boy and his family fled Kit Carson and his white soldiers.'

'What was the great round-up?' Buck had heard of Kit Carson. He had been at one time or another, a scout, a trapper, and a trader. But he was most remembered by instructors at the academy as a colonel in the New Mexico militia that defeated the Confederates on their way through New Mexico in a desperate strike to capture the Union's gold reserves in Colorado.

'Back in 1863,' McBride said, 'Carson and his white soldiers attacked the Navajos, burning their crops and killing their sheep. Most of the Navajo fled into a large canyon similar to this one, but further west, a place called Canyon de Chelly. The Navajos always considered it to be invulnerable, but it wasn't, not against Carson.

'Those Navajos still alive when Carson finished, were rounded up, along with scattered bands and families from other parts of our homeland, and marched to a reservation down on the Pecos. Many died on the walk down. This place was hot, windy and full of mosquitoes. Many more Navajo died there from chicken pox, measles and whooping cough. Worst of all, many died of starvation because the government wouldn't give them any supplies. In 1868, the whites gave it up as a bad idea and let what was left of the Navajo, the survivors who promised to be good Indians, walk home.'

'I'm surprised Joe will even help us,' Buck said. He remembered reading something about the campaign against the Navajos in his history classes. But most of the recent history of the western United States had been over-shadowed by the Civil War. It was still being studied, debated and re-fought by everyone. Only something like the massacre of that idiot Custer had the magnitude to get talked about by his instructors.

'He's not as bitter as some of the other elders,' McBride said. 'Joe's family and a couple of others fled into this canyon and were never found. Here, they lived free, as Navajos were meant to live.'

'So what do we do when we get to this village, make a stand?' Buck couldn't see how that was going to help them.

'No. Joe says that at this village there's a way out of the canyon. It's a path up through the canyon wall, and it's so steep and narrow that you can

213

only go on foot.'

'But even on foot, won't Russell's men still be able to catch us?'

'No,' McBride assured Buck. 'One of Joe's sons is going to meet us with horses at the top of the canyon. Russell and his gang will have to ride back out and around the canyon lands. It will take him a week before he can pick up our trail. By then, we can be back in Sante Fe. They won't dare come there. But first we've got to beat Russell to the end of the canyon and get to the village.'

Buck thought it was a simple but effective plan. He could only see one flaw, and it could be disastrous.

'What if his son's late with the horses?'

McBride laughed at his friend's worries. 'Joe says we can hold off Russell's gang from the top of the trail. They can only come up single file and there's no place to hide from a man with a rifle on top. Russell's men could be held there until that man's ammunition ran out.'

Slowly the four of them picked their way through the maze of canyons, hiding their trail as they went. They turned up what Buck thought were side canyons that opened up on other side canyons. At one point he heard the sound of horses from somewhere, then everything was quiet again.

'Perhaps they lost our trail,' Emily said hopefully.

'Maybe,' McBride said, 'but I don't think so. Hiding our trail might fool Russell's people, but not Black Hand.'

True to his words, they soon heard the sound of horses again. Joe shouted something from up front and turned off into a side canyon. Emily followed. McBride and Buck, however, stopped to untie the brush they had been dragging.

'Joe says we need to speed up now, for a little bit,' McBride said. 'I think the old man's got a plan because he sure doesn't seem to be worried.'

'In his day,' McBride added, 'Joe was one of the best warriors in these parts. Lots of stories about him are still told to kids at night.'

'I hope you're right,' Buck said. He finished untying his brush bundle and then spurred his horse up to catch McBride who was disappearing up the side canyon.

The canyon quickly became narrow and twisting. But, about a half a mile further, it opened out into a wide, straight stretch for 300 or 400 yards before disappearing around another sharp bend. Emily and Joe were waiting in the middle of the wide stretch.

Joe started explaining something to McBride and gesturing at different parts of the canyon wall on both sides. Finally, McBride nodded and turned to Buck.

'We're to wait here for Russell,' McBride said. He pointed ahead to a large mound of rocks near the point where the canyon twisted away from view. 'We can set up there and leave our horses around the bend. We should be able to hold Russell off for an hour or so and then catch up with Emily and Joe.' Buck watched briefly as the old Indian and the girl rode off and then he turned to the business at hand.

The winding section of the canyon they had just come through would have made a good place to stop Russell and his men, but that would have turned into a cat and mouse game with the cat never very far behind. Little time would really be gained. But here, in the middle of this straight section, there were few places a man could take cover. Buck and McBride could use their rifles to pin down Russell and his men, really hurt them, and throw them into confusion. It would take at least an hour for them to get organized and take up their pursuit again.

Buck and McBride hid their horses and came back to their hiding place. Buck was carrying an old canvas feed bag filled with something heavy.

'What's that?' McBride asked.

'A little surprise for Russell and his boys,' Buck told McBride, and reached into the bag and pulled out a short, round red stick and held it up for McBride to see.

'Dynamite!' McBride said. 'OK, but just remember that first I get a crack at that cousin of mine and you must take out Youngblood. That way, the ones most dangerous to us will be gone for sure.'

Buck found a long, stout stick and hurried back down the canyon.

★ ★ ★

Neddy Vanders was a ruined man. So was everyone else riding with Youngblood, and all because of one man: Buck Buchanan. Vanders' initial anger and need for revenge on his old roommate, gave way to an acceptance of what was. Vanders had planned for such a contingency. However, he saw these very same passions eating away at Russell and the others. Vanders knew it would destroy them because none was thinking beyond catching and killing Buchanan and the girl.

Vanders had made plans for just such a disaster. By now, his wife had taken all their money and fled to the West Coast, to San Francisco, to wait for him to join her. He would be able to pick up his life and start over someplace where he could use his talents to make a comfortable living.

Vanders also knew that they might catch his old friend. But killing Buck might prove more costly than they thought. And what would be gained in the end?

Black Hand led them into a narrow, twisty side canyon. Vanders followed at a slow walk, letting others pass him. He noted that the colonel had also slowed up. He waited for Neddy to catch up and they walked their horses along, behind everyone else.

'What do you think, Neddy?'

'This place brings to mind the words of one of my instructors, at the academy. He warned against constricting topography because it's so ideally suited for a small force to ambush a larger party.'

'I agree,' Russell said. 'So, let's tag along behind just in case Buchanan also recalls those words.'

But the others also sensed how dangerous the narrow section of the canyon was. Everyone rode slowly and those in front cautiously turned each corner, expecting at any moment to face rifle fire. But to everyone's relief, they passed through the narrow section without incident and picked up speed when they came to the straight section of the canyon. They were halfway up the long straight stretch when Black Hand reined his horse in. Twenty yards in front of him, in the middle of the canyon, was a long pole stuck in the ground. Something was hanging from the top of the stick.

'What's that?' one of the riders asked.

'Be damned if I know,' Youngblood replied.

They walked their mounts closer.

'It's an old feedbag,' someone said.

When the front riders were a couple of yards from where the stick was stuck in the sand, they stopped and looked at it.

'What in hell's it supposed to mean?' Youngblood asked. He studied the canyon suspiciously. Then at the far end, he saw the glint of sun on metal and a puff of smoke. But it was too late. Before he could say or do anything, Black Hand suddenly threw up his arms and was knocked from his saddle by an unseen blow, followed by the sound of a gunshot. Then more bullets whined by, followed by the sound of gunshots. Youngblood was hit and fell from his horse. At that point, the feedbag exploded. Horses screamed in pain and terror. Riders went down with their mounts. There was general pandemonium as riders leaped from their horses to find cover. Vanders and Russell were quick to do likewise.

At first Buck and McBride concentrated their fire on the riders, keeping them pinned down. Then they shifted from the men to their horses. Several horses were hit and went down kicking and screaming. To Vanders' surprise, it was Deputy Miller who had the quick sense to remount and drive their horses out of gunshot range, back down the canyon.

With Youngblood dead, his men were thrown into confusion. Few even fired back at the ambushers. Then Colonel Russell took command and began organizing the outlaws. He got half of them to fire on the ambushers while the other half advanced. In this way the outlaws worked their way up to the rocks where the ambushers had been. It took them a good half an hour before they stormed the rocks. No one was there. Only Neddy had noticed that there had been no rifle fire coming from behind the rocks for some time.

'Walk back down the canyon,' Russell

told one of the men, 'find Miller and the horses.'

He motioned Neddy to follow him and walked over and sat down on a rock in the shade of the canyon wall. Neddy watched as several men stripped Youngblood and the Navajo of their weapons and emptied out their pockets, haggling amongst themselves over who got what. Others were helping bandage up the several wounded. But five bodies testified to the effectiveness of Buck's ambush.

'Your friend's smart,' Russell told him. 'He hurt us and bought himself at least an extra two hours.'

Neddy was surprised at how calm the colonel was.

'But your friend's efforts are futile.' Russell smiled and said again, almost to himself, 'quite futile, now.'

*　*　*

Several miles from the ambush, Joe Begay led the others around another of the seemingly endless twisting bends in the canyon. But this time, when they rounded the corner, they came out into an immense space a quarter of mile wide and more than a half-mile long. Buck and Emily could only stare. Where the canyon ended, wind and water had carved a massive amphitheater out of the red rock walls. Under this protective overhang, stood a city of stone.

'Nish Tegoni,' McBride said. 'It's one of the largest pueblos built by the old ones.'

They rode closer, and Buck could make out more detail. The ruins were shaped like a giant crescent, with the back built close to the base of the canyon wall, at the back of the amphitheater. The inner part of the crescent was composed of row after row of rooms. Buck thought it looked like some great stone honeycomb. The space between the tips of the crescent formed a large plaza that was paved with flat red sandstone.

Although large chunks of rock, some as large as small houses, had fallen from the ceiling and walls of the amphitheater on to the pueblo below, many of the ruin's stone walls and buildings were still intact. Here and there, graceful towers had been erected, some soaring up hundreds of feet. They kept a silent vigil over the rest of the ruins. High above the ruins, on a wide ledge, was a series of stone rooms built against the canyon wall. Buck could see no way of getting up to them from below. He wondered what their purpose was.

'How many people do you think lived here?' he asked, as they rode toward the ruins.

McBride translated Buck's question for Joe Begay. The old man took off his hat and rubbed his head as if to help himself remember something, then spoke to McBride for several minutes. As he spoke, he gestured at various parts of the ruins.

'He says that he came here several years back with Kenyon Rita, a famous medicine man from before the Long Walk,' McBride translated. 'They counted over two thousand rooms here, but he's not sure that they were all lived in.' McBride pointed to a section of smaller rooms near the front of the pueblo. 'Kenyon Rita thought that a lot of the rooms were used for storing corn and other foods for the winter.' McBride pointed at the long row of rooms built up on the ledge. 'Those may have been used for defense or storage, or both, no one knows. Begay says that a thousand people or more could have lived here.'

'That's as many people as live around Sante Fe,' Emily said. 'What happened to them? Where did they go?'

'No one knows,' McBride said.

They reached the ruins, and Buck saw that they were constructed in the same way as the smaller buildings he and Emily had seen down the canyon, near the cabin. Flat, reddish-tan sandstone rocks had been carefully laid in a mud mortar to form walls. In many places, however, the mud mortar had eroded out, leaving the walls in an unstable condition. Several of the great walls had, over time, fallen and were nothing but large heaps of jumbled stone.

'We have to leave our horses here,' McBride said. 'There's plenty of grass and water for them. I'll come back for them later, that is, if Youngblood's gang doesn't gather them up.'

Buck didn't like having to leave his horses. Alamo, his big dun, had been more than just something to ride, he had also been a companion and friend. He and the horse trusted each other completely.

They unsaddled their mounts and slipped bridles off. McBride and Buck took everything, including packs, and put it down in one of the kivas, a large, covered circular room that had been built into the floor of the plaza. Buck was especially careful in handling a blanket-wrapped, medium-sized box.

'It's the dynamite,' he said, when he

saw McBride's quizzical expression.

McBride took dirt and spread it over their packs so they weren't so noticeable. Then he put some sticks and rubble on top, hiding everything as best he could. 'I'll get all this when I get the horses,' he told Buck.

Joe Begay, who had wandered off toward the right side of the ruins, now called for the others. When Buck got there, he saw that the old man was standing in front of a large crevice in the canyon wall. It was not visible from the front of the ruins. Inside the narrow crack was a steep, natural stone staircase leading upward. Without a word, the old man started up.

Buck noticed fresh cornmeal sprinkled around the entrance to the path. Old Joe had been at work, Buck guessed, making some kind of medicine for them. McBride followed Joe, then Emily. Buck went up last. As they climbed upward, loose rubble dislodged by McBride and Begay clattered down on Buck and Emily, making climbing difficult.

The crevice with its steep trail led upward for several hundred feet, to a ledge with a row of rooms built along it. There the crevice narrowed to form a foot-wide gap between the back of the ledge and the canyon wall. On this wall, the old ones had scratched deeply into the sandstone to create crude outlines of deer, turkey, and bighorn sheep. There were also outlines of strange, bird-like creatures playing flutes, and countless abstract geometric designs scratched into the soft rock.

Joe Begay, who was leading the way through the rooms, stopped suddenly, said something to McBride, and pointed out one of the small, square windows built into the wall. Buck looked to where the old man was pointing and saw a large group of riders coming slowly up the canyon. Russell!

'Where do we go from here?' Emily asked.

Joe Begay heard the fear in her voice and walked back to her. He laid a reassuring hand on her arm and said something very gently in Navajo to her.

'He says that at the end of this ledge, the crevice opens up again and there's another trail that leads up through the wall to the rim of the canyon,' McBride translated. They hurried along behind the old Indian and, just as he had promised, at the end of the ledge they found another break in the canyon wall and a trail leading up.

They had gone only thirty or forty yards when, as they rounded a bend in the trail, they came to a sheer wall of loose rock, a hundred feet high, wedged into the crack and blocking their way. Everyone stared in disbelief. Buck pushed his way past the others and tried to climb up the obstruction, but the small rocks pulled loose when he grasped them, causing him to fall back down on to the path. Only McBride voiced what the other three were thinking.

'We're trapped!'

10

Neddy spurred his horse up to the front of the riders. Colonel Russell was now leading the men and was setting a slow pace. The far end of the canyon and a massive set of ruins were now in sight.

'Well, Neddy,' Russell said, as the younger man caught up with him, 'I do believe we have them this time.' Neddy saw that his boss was smiling expansively. 'Our Indian friend told Youngblood that there was a trail out of here, up through some cracks in the canyon wall.'

'Won't they have fled up it by now?' Neddy was puzzled.

'There's their horses,' a rider shouted. Neddy saw five horses moving through the sage-brush toward a small spring of water issuing forth near the canyon wall. A small creek flowed from a pool of water formed by the spring and trickled down the floor of the canyon for several hundred yards before disappearing into the sandy soil.

'In answer to your question, Neddy,' the colonel said, 'according to our late guide, the way was blocked by a landslide, a couple of years ago. And I'll bet Buchanan's Indian friends didn't know that until today!'

'Then Buck will have to make a stand,' Neddy said, more to himself than to Russell.

'Yes,' the older man said. His mind recalled other times when he had led men into battle. As he looked at the massive stone ruins, he wished he had just one of his artillery pieces here. It would be fun to demolish the stone structure, room by room, floor by floor, and bury Buchanan and the girl under tons of rock.

'We'll stop over there.' Russell pointed to a small rise in the canyon floor. 'It should be out of range of rifle fire.'

Neddy sent two men to gather up the fugitives' horses. The rest of the party stopped on the small rise and sat surveying the ruins.

'Send some men forward to the ruins,' Russell directed, 'and draw their fire so we'll know where they are.'

Neddy and Russell watched as three riders left the knoll and rode toward the huge stone structure. Suddenly one of the riders fell from his horse and lay still, a second had his horse shot out from under him. In a daring feat of bravery, the third rider wheeled his mount back and rode through a hail of bullets and picked up the man who had been unhorsed. Everyone on the small rise cheered as they rode out of the fugitives' rifle range.

'They're in the ruins up on that small ledge overlooking the main structure,' Russell said. He continued to study the ruins through his glasses. 'There is a tall structure, a tower from the looks of it, whose top floor is almost level with Buchanan's ledge. We can keep them pinned down from there while some of our men find the path to the ledge and make their way up.'

Russell put his field-glasses back in their case. 'I think we have them right where we want. Tomorrow, before it gets light, we'll move into the ruins and flush them out at sunrise.' He paused to light a cigar. 'Have the men set up camp here and post a line of guards across the canyon floor to ensure that none of Buchanan's party slip out tonight.'

* * *

'What are they doing now?' Emily asked.

'Just waiting.' Buck sat where he could see over a partially collapsed wall and was reloading his rifle. 'They know where we are now and are setting up a camp on the little knoll out in the middle of the canyon floor.'

'But what are they waiting for?' Her voice was edged with fear.

'For dark.' Buck went over to Emily and sat down beside her. He pulled her close and held her.

'Tonight when it's dark, they'll move into the ruins below and wait for daylight. Then they'll try and take us.' He knew that he didn't need to tell her how desperate their situation was. The minutes stretched into hours until finally the sun sank behind the canyon wall. McBride came in.

'Where's old Joe?' Buck asked.

'That old man's just sitting in front of the rock slide, praying and chanting for some way over it. He says this is a sacred place and we won't die here.'

'Do you think we might be able to slip out of here tonight, in the dark?'

'I could, but I don't think Joe will leave the crack in the wall. He really believes that his gods will save us.' McBride grinned. 'And since that old man's my grandpa, I don't think I can go off and leave him up here.'

'Let him be, then,' Buck told McBride.

Buck thought he could also slip by the outlaws and escape. But it would be too difficult a task for Emily. So, like his friend McBride, he would also stay.

'How are you fixed for ammunition?' he asked McBride.

'I only have a few rounds left. I didn't think we would have to stand and fight and didn't bring a lot. But there's a bandoleer in my saddle-bags and I'm going down to the kiva and get it. Want me to bring your saddle-bags up?'

'Yes. And any canteens that are down there. We'll need water.'

'There's a small spring at the base of the cliff, behind the wall of the pueblo. I'll fill all the canteens I can find. Maybe I can find some whole pots in the ruins to bring up more water.' With that, McBride slipped out.

'Do we have a chance, to get out I mean?' Emily's eyes were full of tears. She had listened intently to Buck and McBride's discussion.

'There's always a chance,' Buck told her, 'but it is a very slim one, I'm afraid.'

'Why does it have to be this way?' Emily started crying and Buck drew her close and held her. There was nothing he could say to her, nothing that would make it any easier for her.

★ ★ ★

Neddy woke suddenly. One of the lookouts was shaking him.

'It's two o'clock,' the man said and left.

Neddy got up and folded his blanket over his saddle and then went to find Russell. The colonel was standing at the edge of the circle of light cast by the campfire, his back to it and he stared out into the dark. A quarter moon had risen over the east canyon wall.

'It's time, sir,' Neddy called to him.

'What? Oh, yes.' Russell turned and walked back to the fire. 'I want a couple of men to stay here, at the outposts, just in case Buchanan and his people try to slip out while we're moving in.' Russell paused, thinking.

'Whertman and two other men have gone ahead into the ruins to scout out the tower and to find the trail up to the ledge. Four from here will come with me to the tower. You take the rest with you and meet Whertman over on the right side of the ruins. He can show you the way up to the ledge. Understood?'

'Yes, sir,' Neddy said.

'It will start at six thirty. By then it should be light enough to shoot.'

Neddy made the necessary assignments and then Russell left first with his party. Neddy and his men followed a few minutes later. There was just enough moonlight for them to make out the dark shapes of choya cactus that seemed to grow everywhere in the gloom of the overhanging cliffs. But every now and then, Neddy would hear someone curse softly under his breath as the man brushed against the outstretched arms of an unseen cactus. More than once, Neddy himself felt the red-hot stinging jab of choya spines.

In spite of these difficulties, they made steady progress and could finally make out the walls of the ruins. But as they came to the walls, Neddy stepped into a hole and fell heavily, wrenching his ankle.

'Are you all right?' someone behind him asked softly.

'Yes, I think so,' he told a shadowy form behind him. He felt hands grasp him and he was helped to his feet and managed to hobble quietly into the ruins.

* * *

Buck sat dozing with his chin on his chest, by one of the small windows, which looked out over the pueblo below. Emily was a few feet away, asleep on the cold stone floor. Something woke Buck, he wasn't sure what, but from the ruins below, came a great crash as somewhere a building collapsed. The noise woke Emily. In the moonlight coming in through the window, Buck could see her sit up suddenly and could make out the fear on her face.

'Buck . . . ' she called, looking around for him.

'Something fell,' Buck told her. 'Everything's OK.' A dark figure stalked in from the direction of the path from below.

'What happened?' Buck asked McBride, who had been standing guard at the top of the path.

'I think a piece of the overhang came loose and fell into the pueblo,' he said and then looked beyond Buck and Emily to the other end of the room. Joe Begay materialized out of the dark end and, in a voice filled with emotion, said something to McBride.

'Old Joe says that was a warning from the Old Ones,' McBride translated. 'This is sacred ground where the gods themselves once walked. And they are angry as hell at Russell and his gang for bringing hate and fear here, coming to kill.'

Begay disappeared back into the darkness and a few minutes later they heard soft chanting coming from the break in the rock.

'What's he doing?' Emily asked.

'Praying,' McBride said, 'like he has all night. He keeps asking the gods to open the pathway out of here and to destroy Russell and the others.'

'Do you believe all that stuff, Charlie?' Buck asked. Although Begay's chanting was soft and low, there was a power to it, a cadence that seemed to match the power and rhythm of the canyon and the earth itself.

'One time I didn't, when I first moved back with my mom's people.' McBride sat quietly for a few seconds then went on, 'A lot has happened since then and I've seen a lot of things that can't be explained. Maybe Old Joe can talk to the gods, I just don't know. But I won't ever again say he can't.'

* * *

There was no dawn deep in the canyon. It simply became lighter and lighter. Neddy was watching the stars as they faded from view, but his mind was elsewhere. He was thinking of his days at West Point, of how he and Buck had enjoyed themselves, sharing the hazing from upper-classmen, the friendly competition for grades and promotions, and the long talks about dreams and ambitions.

Two months ago, a fortune seemed to have been within his reach. Now it was gone and he was a fugitive, ruined. Even if they killed Buck, he would have to leave, to go somewhere else and start over. Russell spoke of fleeing to California or Alaska. But Neddy knew of a better place that was still ninety per cent wilderness, a place where there was land to be had and fortunes to be made.

'I've found a path.' Whertman came into the roofless room where Neddy and the others in his group waited. 'It goes up through a break in the canyon wall, just behind the main ruins. Only place it can go is up to that ledge.' Whertman was smiling. At last he was going to be able to get at that bastard, Buchanan.

'But that's not all,' Whertman said. He held up a small blanket-wrapped bundle. 'We found Buchanan's dynamite! We saw someone climb out of one of those big holes in the ground in the ruins and we watched which way he went. That's how we found the trail up to the ledge.

'Buchanan had stashed his gear down in the hole. Whoever it was must have been getting more ammo.' Whertman held up the bundle. 'Whoever it was is going to wish they hadn't forgotten this!'

'Excellent,' Neddy said. With the dynamite they could blow up the ruins on the ledge and everyone in it. Suddenly he wanted nothing to do with this, with Buck's death. 'Take the men over to where it starts. I'll be along in a minute. I want to wrap my ankle.' He pulled out his bandanna. 'We'll move up to the ledge once the colonel's men open fire.'

Whertman gathered up those in the room and left. Neddy had glimpses of them moving back through the ruins. He wrapped his bandanna tightly around his swollen ankle and hobbled to the door.

'Sorry, Buck,' he said softly, as he looked up at the ledge. Neddy hobbled out the door and away from the ruins. If he hurried, he thought to himself, he could get to the horses before the shooting started.

★ ★ ★

As Buck kept watch out of the small, narrow window, night began to fade and the canyon slowly filled with light. He glanced across the room and saw Emily asleep on the floor. Near her were several old pots McBride had filled with water and brought up. The large clay containers were a light gray with wide bands of geometric designs around their middles.

As he studied the vessels, he couldn't

help but wonder about the people who had made them. Did it end this way for them, in a shower of arrows? Is that why the city was deserted? Did some other man, long ago, look across this room at his woman asleep, there on the floor, and realize that their time together was almost at an end? Is this what happened to Nish Tegoni, cutthroats like Russell and his men came into the canyon, like snakes entering paradise? Or did that man and his woman escape up the path that was now blocked?

Buck shook his head to clear his mind of such thoughts. He turned his attention back to the ruins. Somewhere in the pueblo below, were Russell and his men. Buck was sure they had moved in under the cover of darkness and were awaiting daylight before trying to take the ledge.

McBride stuck his head in the doorway. 'There's someone at the foot of the trail. It's about to start. I'll hold them off when they try and come up.'

'How long do you think you can hold them?'

'Until I run out of shells,' McBride shrugged.

'Then it's just a matter of time,' Buck said. Until now there had been a small sliver of hope in the back of his mind. Something might happen, a lucky break of some kind that would allow them to escape from this trap. But with the coming of the day, it was getting harder and harder to hold on to any hope.

'Yes, but we can make it cost them a hell of a lot,' McBride said. And then he smiled suddenly. 'But don't forget old Joe's gods.' Then McBride disappeared back out the door.

Buck turned his attention back to the ruins. He gave a start as he saw someone moving in the tall tower that rose up from the ruins, to almost the level of the ledge. Then a harsh voice called to him.

'Buchanan! Buchanan, can you hear me?'

'What do you want?' Buck shouted back.

'You can't get away this time! You might as well come out and give yourselves up. We'll let the Indians go!'

As if in reply, Buck heard McBride open fire on someone on the path.

Then Buck saw a man in one of the tower windows. He was aiming a rifle at the ledge. Before the man could shoot, Buck put his rifle sights on him and pulled the trigger. The man in the window threw up his arms and pitched forward out of the window into the ruins below.

Rifle fire suddenly poured forth from all the windows in the top floor of the tower. While most of the outlaw's bullets hit the outer wall, many came through the window and struck the rock walls only to ricochet off and whine about the room. Emily was awake and looking about wildly.

'Stay down, flat!' Buck yelled, over the noise of the shooting and whining bullets.

A round hit the rock wall just a few inches from Buck's head, sending fragments of rock flying. One piece hit Buck in the forehead, knocking him to the floor. Emily, seeing him go down, screamed and started toward him. But Buck sat up, blood streaming down his face.

'No,' he yelled when he saw her coming across the room, 'stay down flat!'

But Emily was oblivious to the bullets. Her man was hurt and she was determined to go to him. Miraculously, she got to him without being hit by the lead whizzing everywhere. Emily knelt down by him and ripped off a small piece of her skirt to wipe the blood from his face. 'It probably needs stitches.'

She tore off more petticoats and bandaged his head. As she did so, the shooting stopped abruptly, the echoes of the last shots rolling down the canyon.

'Probably letting their barrels cool,'

Buck said, in reply to her questioning look.

After the roar of all the shooting, the stillness made Emily nervous and she shuddered involuntarily. At that moment, Joe Begay walked into the room. He didn't crouch down so as to avoid presenting a target for Russell's men, but stood tall and proud. He said something to Buck and Emily and then pointed toward the break in the canyon wall where the path to the top was. He motioned for them to go there.

'Why? It's still blocked, isn't it?' Buck asked, but the old man didn't hear. He was already hurrying out toward his grandson.

'I wonder what . . . ' Buck was saying when McBride and Begay rushed back into the room.

'Get out of here, get off the ledge!' McBride shouted. 'Get up the pathway, quick! Old Joe's been talking to his gods and says this place is going to be destroyed any minute! I don't know why, but I believe him.'

Suddenly the shooting started up again and bullets began to whine about the room. Begay left the room while McBride helped Emily up and they ran out after him. Buck was the last out, and at the start of the path, he happened to glance back into the room. Through the far door, he could see Whertman and others coming up on to the ledge.

Whertman heaved something into the room and the outlaws all ducked down. It was a bundle of dynamite with a lit fuse stuck into it. They had found his dynamite. But the bundle of dynamite sticks hit the floor of the room and rolled to the back of the ledge and into the wide crack there.

Buck had just enough time to dart around the corner and leap up the narrow passageway. He felt the walls of the crevice shift and heard a thunderous explosion from the direction of the ledge. Then came a low, powerful rumbling from the ruins below. He thought he heard men screaming.

Just as suddenly as it started, the canyon was quiet except for the occasional crash of loose rocks falling from the walls. Buck looked out of the crack in the wall. A few feet below, where the ledge had once been, there was nothing but empty space.

'It's gone!' he shouted up to the others. 'The ledge, the tower, everything, it's all fallen!'

McBride climbed back down the path to Buck. It was then that they noticed that the deep crevice where they were, had widened. Where there had only been room for one man before the explosion, they could now stand shoulder to shoulder. Then both men looked back at the ruins.

'The ledge must have taken the tower with it when it fell,' McBride said. He looked around and saw other places where loose slabs of rock had been jolted by the explosion and fell into the ruins.

'Then Russell and his gang . . . ?'

'Are buried down there by all that

rock.' McBride looked at Buck. 'Old Joe was right. His gods did get 'em!'

Buck thought it more likely it was the dynamite and all of the fissures and cracks running everywhere through the canyon's weathered walls, that had caused so many huge pieces of rock to fall from the canyon wall and overhang.

There was a shout from up the path. Emily was waving excitedly for them to come up. Buck and McBride scrambled up the steep trail and caught up with her.

'Look!' she said, and pointed to the wall of rubble. The shock of the blast had shifted the walls enough so that a small tunnel had formed beneath the wall of rubble wedged into the crevice. Begay was nowhere in sight.

'He went up through it and then came back and motioned for us to come.' Then she crawled into it and disappeared.

Buck was the last to go into the small tunnel. It was a tight squeeze and more than once he felt himself stuck. A wave of fear washed over him, brought on he knew by claustrophobia. Spurred on then by a mild panic, Buck clawed his way through. At last, he pulled himself out of the narrow passageway and into the open on the far side. Emily was waiting for him, her dress was torn and dirty and she had cuts and scrapes on her arms and legs.

'We're free!' she said. Tears ran down her cheeks and she came to Buck. He held her tightly for several minutes, until she pulled away, and they started for the top.

* * *

One fall day, a year and a half later, Buck rode in from Sante Fe. It was late in the day and he saw smoke streaming out of the kitchen chimney. He knew his wife was inside getting dinner. He took his horse to the corrals and unsaddled the big dun, turning it loose. Alamo promptly rolled in the dirt and then went to feed from a rack of hay.

Buck hung his saddle in the tack room and walked to the house and stopped on the front porch. There he leaned against a porch column and watched the sunset. The dying sun became a fiery, orange-red orb as it sank behind the thin, dark line of mountains to the south-west. Buck made it a habit to stop here each evening and watch the day end.

The last of the brilliant yellow leaves had fallen from the huge old cotton-woods that towered above the house. A chilly evening breeze swirled the leaves about the ground like a giant, unseen hand. Buck came out of his reverie and went inside.

He walked through the outer rooms, back to the kitchen. There, standing at the stove was his wife. He walked up behind her and slid his arms around her.

'How was your trip?' Emily asked.

'Fine. I sold the lambs for three dollars a head more than I expected.' Buck had taken over running Emily's dad's sheep business and had bought a lot more land to add to it. He and Emily now had one of the largest sheep and cattle operations in the territory.

Buck walked over to a wooden cradle suspended from the ceiling in the corner. The cradle had been a gift from Charlie McBride. Buck looked down into it, at the baby inside. Charles Ernest Buchanan was sound asleep.

'We have a letter,' Buck said, pulling it out of his pocket and giving it to Emily. The letter was post-marked 'Australia'.

'Who do we know there?' She studied the envelope. 'And there's no return address. Who is it from?'

'Open it and find out.'

Emily did as she was told. Inside were just a few, brief lines:

> *Calamity and happiness . . . in all cases*
> *They are men's own seeking.*
> *Wishing you the best,*
>
> > *Neddy*

We do hope that you have enjoyed reading this large print book.

Did you know that all of our titles are available for purchase?

We publish a wide range of high quality large print books including:
Romances, Mysteries, Classics
General Fiction
Non Fiction and Westerns

Special interest titles available in large print are:
The Little Oxford Dictionary
Music Book, Song Book
Hymn Book, Service Book

Also available from us courtesy of Oxford University Press:
Young Readers' Dictionary
(large print edition)
Young Readers' Thesaurus
(large print edition)

For further information or a free brochure, please contact us at:
Ulverscroft Large Print Books Ltd.,
The Green, Bradgate Road, Anstey,
Leicester, LE7 7FU, England.
Tel: (00 44) **0116 236 4325**
Fax: (00 44) **0116 234 0205**

BENDER'S BOOT

Mark Bannerman

Bloody Kansas, 1872, and Conroy McClure is searching for his missing brother. At a remote inn, he becomes involved with an evil family and, in particular, the she-devil of a daughter who ensnares men in a murderous web of sensuality. Local vigilantes storm the inn, intent on lynching the entire family. But the killers have fled, taking McClure with them. Buried in the adjacent orchard are twelve brutally mutilated bodies, including a little girl who was clearly buried alive. But what is the fate of Conroy McClure?